DEEDS
OF
WISDOM

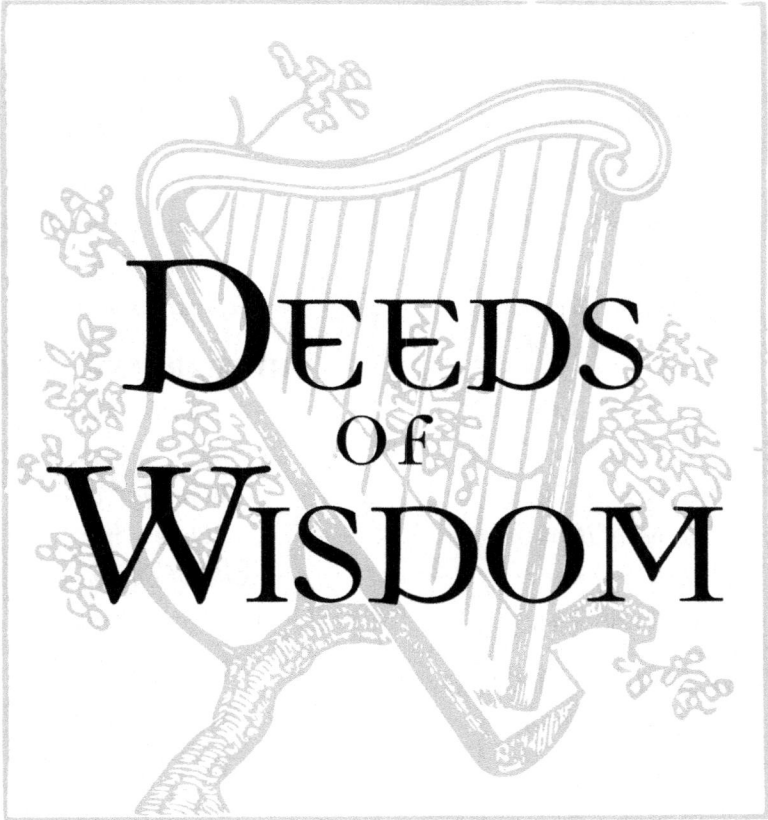

paksenarrion world chronicles iii

ALSO BY ELIZABETH MOON

STANDALONE NOVELS
Speed of Dark
Remnant Population

THE DEED OF PAKSENARRION
Sheepfarmer's Daughter
Divided Allegiance
Oath of Gold

PALADIN'S LEGACY
Oath of Fealty
Kings of the North
Echoes of Betrayal
Limits of Power
Crown of Renewal

THE LEGACY OF GIRD
Surrender None
Liar's Oath

VATTA'S WAR
Trading in Danger
*Marque and Reprisal^*
Engaging the Enemy
Command Decision
Victory Conditions

^ UK title: *Moving Target*

VATTA'S PEACE
Cold Welcome
Into the Fire

PLANET PIRATES
(with Anne McCaffrey)
Sassinak
Generation Warriors

THE SERRANO LEGACY
Hunting Party
Sporting Chance
Winning Colors
Once a Hero
Rules of Engagement
Change of Command
Against the Odds

SHORT STORY COLLECTIONS
Lunar Activity
Phases
Moon Flights
Deeds of Honor
Deeds of Youth
Deeds of Wisdom

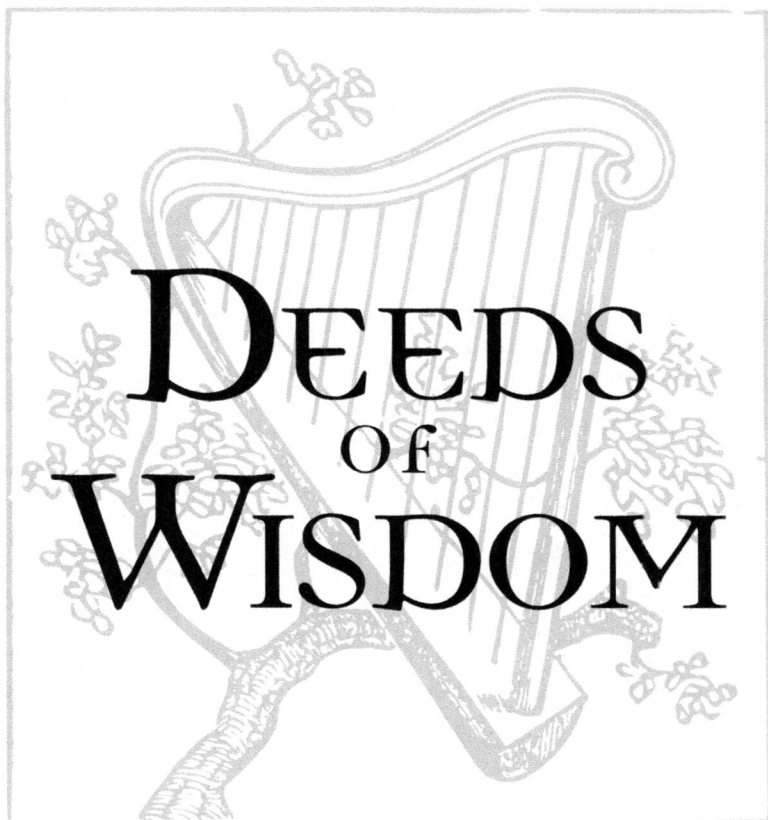

Deeds
of
Wisdom

paksenarrion world chronicles III

Elizabeth Moon

JAB
Published by JABberwocky Literary Agency, Inc.

Deeds of Wisdom: Paksenarrion World Chronicles III
Copyright © 2025 by Elizabeth Moon
All Rights Reserved

Collected for the first time by JABberwocky Literary Agency, Inc., in 2025.

ISBN (paperback) 978-1-625677-95-2
ISBN (ebook) 978-1-625677-94-5

Cover design by Tara O'Shea

Interior design by Lisa Rodgers

1. "In the Valley of Death" – first published in *Deeds of Wisdom*. Copyright © 2025 by Elizabeth Moon.
2. "My Princess" – first published in *Warrior Princesses*, 1998, DAW Books, ed. Elizabeth Ann Scarborough and Martin H. Greenberg. Copyright © 1988 by Elizabeth Moon.
3. "The Shepherd's Tale" – first published in *Deeds of Wisdom*. Copyright © 2025 by Elizabeth Moon.
4. "Judgment" – first published in *The Dragon Quintet*, Tor Books, 2003, ed. Marvin Kaye, reprinted in *Moon Flights*. Copyright © 2003 by Elizabeth Moon.
5. "Final Honor" – first published in *Deeds of Wisdom*. Copyright © 2025 by Elizabeth Moon.
6. "Destiny" – first published in *Deeds of Wisdom*. Copyright © 2025 by Elizabeth Moon.

For the latest updates about Elizabeth's novels, and everything related to *The Deed of Paksenarrion*, *Paladin's Legacy*, *The Legacy of Gird*, *Vatta's War*, and *The Serrano Legacy* series, as well as her standalone novels, visit her on the web http://www.elizabethmoon.com or the Paksworld blog http://www.paksworld.com/blog.

All characters and events in this publication, other than those in the public domain, are fictitious and any resemblance to real persons, living or dead, is purely coincidental.

Published by JABberwocky Literary Agency, Inc.
49 W. 45th Street, Suite #5N
New York, NY 10036
awfulagent.com/ebooks

CONTENTS

AUTHOR'S NOTE ON
DEEDS OF WISDOM &
"IN THE VALLEY OF DEATH"

What, you may wonder, are "deeds" of Wisdom? Isn't wisdom more cerebral, less active? Well… not exactly. We speak of "wise words," and words uttered are deeds. People in these stories say things, and do things, which approach different aspects of wisdom (and some folly) at work.

The roots of "In the Valley of Death" go deep into the history of Paksworld, a part of it not yet explored in the books: Old Aare and what it was like in the many thousands of years that preceded the familiar world of Paksenarrion's first adventures. At this time, empires and nation-states and city-states had risen and fallen; wars had been fought and peaceful trade restored, many times. But also at this time, the Great Dryness was spreading, sparking more wars, and throwing together peoples who could not find any common ground.

Publication Note: "In the Valley of Death" is new, written exclusively for *Deeds of Wisdom*.

IN THE VALLEY OF DEATH

Serendola stared at the long low ridge of land that lay between his troop and the higher forested hills beyond. "We did not need this," he said.

Between where they stood and the ridge, the ground grew steadily rockier.

Nobody answered. They were all hungry, thirsty, exhausted, near half of them walking wounded and three worse-wounded jammed together in a handcart under a bloodied cloak as the best that could be done for them.

Serendola knew Krikhol, worst wounded of the three, unconscious when loaded on the cart, would almost certainly die by sundown. Behind their troop, the relentless new Emperor pursued any who had ever refused his orders, and his troops were less than a day behind.

"I'll go look." Castrin, second-in-command, started off for the hump, the mass of rocks and scrub and low trees that stretched exactly across their only chance of safety, the forested hills beyond. He walked faster, no longer pushing the cart.

Going around that hump, Serendola knew, would take too long. Maybe Castrin could find a way through. Maybe they would all die here.

"Rest," Serendola said. "Half a sun-hand." Most of the troop sat where they had stood. Would they get up again? He had no idea why they still did what he told them, when it was clear so many of his decisions had been wrong. Maybe just habit? His own habits took him to the handcart where the three wounded men lay protected from the sun by the cloak spread over all three of them.

Krikhol *had* died. Agkert and Menis stared at him, wordless, when he felt Krikhol's neck for the life-beat and found nothing. Serendola shook his head; expecting that death made it no less painful. They knew, of course. They said nothing when he took his hand away. What could anyone say?

Serendola pulled Krikhol's body from the cart and carried it away from the group before laying it straight on the grass. He looked around. If he could find stones, he could pile them… maybe… It would take time.

Movement caught his eye. Sooner than he'd expected, Castrin clambered down the near slope of the hump and waved, jogging. Serendola sighed and walked toward him.

"It was a city once, I think." Castrin said when he was near enough. "Big stones—some carved designs—trees growing out of holes between them. We might be able to hide in there. Awhile, anyway."

"Did you find a hidden farm with fruit on the trees and grain in the barn?" Serendola asked. Then he shook his head. "I'm sorry. Unfair. I just… Krikhol died."

"We can at least bury him there," Castrin said. "I did see two fruit trees but no fruit." Of course no fruit, this time of year. "I'll help you carry him," Castrin said.

Serendola turned back to the others—the blank-eyed, exhausted others, now looking at him as if he should conjure bread and meat and water out of the air itself. "Tell them, Castrin," he said. Castrin repeated what he had said before. Then Serendola added his own assessment. "It is die here, in the open, when they come upon us—tonight or tomorrow, most likely—or go up that slope, into those broken stones and scrub. They will search. Some may escape, for a time. I give no orders: choose."

Then he went to the handcart, where the two worst wounded lay under a stained cloak. Agkert and Menis, cousins, friends of his childhood...

"We can carry you up there," he said. "But the cart won't make it."

"Is there shade?" Agkert asked.

"Pretty girls?" Menis asked.

"Shade, yes. And some shelter."

The two looked at each other.

"I'd risk it for shade," Agkert said.

"Not even *ugly* girls?" Menis said, and coughed. Menis, who had once shared a queen's bed though he was never a king. Beautiful Menis, he had been called, before the wounds that made him a thing to shudder at.

"No girls," Serendola said. "Just shade."

"Where there's shade, there's bound to be water," Agkert said. "Come, cousin. At least it will be more difficult for the Emperor's minions."

"You are cruel," Menis said, "but I will go, that you not be lonely in the dark." He coughed again. "And to make it more difficult for the Emperor's minions, Esea darken their light."

Serendola had no energy to curse the Emperor or his minions. He turned to the others, and most got up—slowly, so slowly—and they took the two men out of the cart, broke it up, fashioned litters from the wood, and carried the two wounded and one dead up the sides of the long mound. The ground was uneven and progress very slow, taking up the rest of the day as tired men, weakened by hunger, struggled over and around obstacles that once would have been easy for them. When the tail of the troop entered the welcome shade of the trees, Serendola looked back. Late-afternoon sun winked on the foremost spear-points of their pursuers, the rest hidden in the dust cloud they raised between distant hills.

In the shade, little currents of cooler air moved, and the change from unending sun eased his eyes. He made his way forward, speaking softly to the men, urging them on to find "a good place, more hidden than that" when he found anyone sprawled in the open. Once at the high point of the mound, he shed his weapons and climbed a tree, hoping to spy out something more useful, though he was certain the gods had deserted them utterly. The good gods, at least.

From the tree branch he saw how narrow the mound was— or mounds, rather, each just touching the next to make what had seemed a single long narrow shape down-valley. He thought back to the barrows he had seen elsewhere. This was bigger, the mounds wider.

A pretty place to build a city, he thought, though far off any trade routes he knew, and an odd shape as well. To the north, across another grassy plain, forested slopes rose higher.

If they could have crossed the valley in a sun-hand or two well before mid-morning that day, if they could have made it up those steeper slopes into the forest, perhaps they could have escaped their pursuers, but he knew it was hopeless. They had lost too much. Whatever happened would happen there.

* * *

In the deepening dusk, he encouraged those who could still move to work their way along the crest of the mound to disperse, find the deepest holes, in hopes some would survive tomorrow's carnage. They had no way to make a stand, as they had made stands before and retreated from one to another, each time losing more men, more supplies, until now… every man still had a knife, but many had no other weapon.

"I'd rather die with my friends," said one after another. Only a few chose to try their luck alone.

Evening cooled the air. Darkness thickened; Serendola stumbled in a hole whose depth he had not judged, and barked his shin on a tree root. Finally he found his way back to his closest friends and crouched on a moss-covered boulder above them—Castrin, Agkert, Menis, Juvan, Soldin, others nearby—and watched for the distant campfires. There—finally—they were, red-winking in the dark. *They* would have food and drink, a night's sleep in comfort before they attacked in the morning.

He slid down the rock to join the others.

"Satisfied?" Agkert asked.

"To be with you, always," he said. Castrin's hand clasped his shoulder.

"We should sing," Menis said. Serenola could hear the wet sound in his lungs, but Menis would sing until he died, or try to. "We should sing all those songs the Emperor wants to silence."

"*All* those songs?" Agkert said. "It will take more than one night."

"The Elder Singers say time singing does not exist," Menis said. "And when I heard them, I thought the same."

"And then your stomach rumbled and they stopped and looked at you," Agkert said. A few men chuckled. "But, cousin, I agree; let us sing while we can and be free while we can."

A chill breath came from the ground, as if it breathed winter on them. Serendola shivered, but no one else seemed to notice.

Menis began, in his labored voice, starting the old marching song they'd been taught as youngsters. Everyone knew it, and singing it again raised spirits though it could do nothing for their situation. That song shifted naturally into the chant of the kings of Fuarr, the list of them all as far back as anyone knew.

Serendola shivered again as chill air filled the hollow in which the two wounded men lay and he and a few others now sat. Menis coughed; the chant paused to wait for him. "Cold," he said. "Something… blessed Lady, is it winter?"

No. Sing.

Serendola jerked as if prodded with a hot needle. "Did you hear that?" he asked.

"Sing," Menis repeated. "Someone wants us to sing? Well, then…" And he took up the chant where he'd left off, with Colrador who built a dam and Vasildor his son who planted five hundred trees.

A faint glow, just enough to see the dark bubble beside Menis's mouth, rose from the moss in the hollow. Serendola leaned forward and wiped the blood away, singing of Padolk who tamed a spotted cat as tall as his hip, and Rethvin who died of fever. He lifted Menis's shoulders and laid Menis's head on his own breast. The ominous gurgle eased, and Menis sang again, of Parwin who started the Golden Tower, and Coldanil and Visran and Rethan who added to it and Bilthan who finished it and set the sun-stone on its top, to light the land in times of danger. Sometime later, when others had taken up the list, and Menis had fallen silent but still breathed, the glow rose, and thickened, and took shape.

The chant stopped in the middle of Borthlun's verse as if cut with a knife. There before them, clear and sharp as a carving in crystal, stood the appearance of a man, every feature distinct, a man as tall as Serendola.

You mourn your king. You sing his lineage. Who then is your new king?

"The king is dead, and all his lineage," Serendola said. It was not—quite—true, but it would be, long before dawn. "All the princes of the blood—" His voice failed for an instant. "And the queen and the princesses as well. We were overcome."

And yet you live.

"For this night," Serendola said. "Death comes with the sun; our enemies are in sight."

And yet you sing.

Serendola shrugged.

"Should a man whimper before Death and the Long Sleep? Song is a flame in the dark. Had we a king, and were he dying here, we would sing him to his grave."

Do you know whose sleep you disturb?

He glanced around; the eyes of his companions gleamed in the wraith's light, but none of them answered. "No," he said.

Once this was King's Rest, where kings came to sleep amid their companions.

Serendola's skin prickled. He had heard something, an old legend, from a tale—teller in the marketplace, but this was no legend. The barrows he'd seen before had been family tombs, not royal ones. The kings of Fuarr had been burned, returned to the Sun in cleansing fire.

Time and time, that sleep was broken, and the last time, the Evil Ones broke into the chambers of rest and scattered the bones, even the bones over which you chose to stay this night. We swore revenge on all who violate the fane.

"We will be bones ourselves ere long," Serendola said. "If you wish revenge, take it: our enemies will thank you."

Silence for a time. Then: *Tell me of your king who died.*

King Teriond's song had not been written; they had no bard but Menis, and Menis now breathed the harsh breaths of one walking the last path into Death itself.

"Teriond the brave," Serendola said, seeing in his mind that figure in his armor, astride his battle steed. "Teriond, who foresaw the change in the world in dreams, waves of sand engulfing the grass, and did his best to hold disaster at bay. He made peace with all who wanted peace, but some who wanted peace nonetheless took service with one who did not. Who wanted only conquest. We of the King's Guard—there were once a thousand of us, arrayed in ten companies, bright with armor and banners, but our enemies had a hand to our thumb, and strong as a thumb is, a hand is stronger."

He died in battle?

"No, alas. He died of poison handed him by an ally who had turned against him. At that same meal also died both his elder sons, commanders of companies. The next morning, we were thrown back, for no one knew who should take command overall, and we who held even small authority had been up all the night."

Serendola went on with the whole sorry tale and felt the weight of it on him again, every moment of every day through the long defeat. The deaths, the wounds, the noise and stench and choking dust, the loss of all that kept them fighting as a coherent army, that broke them into separate units, each struggling vainly like a hirk-beetle turned on its back.

He stopped when he came to the loss of the city, the death of the queen, the torn bodies in the palace they had fought so hard and so hopelessly to save. They had been outflanked; they came too late, and the enemy had backed away, letting them see what was lost. "Forgive me," he said, his voice thick with tears. "I cannot say more now. Let us sing again, if we can, and go to Death with stout hearts."

Light strengthened; more wraiths appeared. Nine he saw now, the kingly one who had come first and eight others. Four men, four women, all in ghostly armor. Behind them ghostly horses, saddled and bridled for war.

You ask nothing.

"Let us sing again," Serendola repeated.

I offer a bargain. Aid for aid.

What aid could a wraith need that a live man could give? He asked, despite his doubts. "What is your bargain?"

When last this place was ruined, some came into our chamber and disturbed our bones. Come down and set them in order, and we will harry your enemies and keep them away.

Serendola shrugged. "I have friends here who need me for this night," he said. "And our enemies will be here in the morning."

Menis's head stirred on his breast. "Do... it..." Menis said, each word on a separate breath.

"Yes," Agkert said. "For all of us."

We will care for your dying.

"Show me," Serendola said. Before he could call another to support Menis's shoulders, cold arms slid under his, cradled Menis, and more cold arms pulled him away. "Menis!" he said, but Menis did not answer. The arms that held Menis looked gentle; a wraith's chill hand caressed his brow.

Serendola stood with the aid of the arms that held him and looked around at the troop. "I will do what I can," he said.

All come.

"All? Why? I said I will do it."

Many bones. Much to do.

He looked at the troop again. "Menis is dying. Agkert needs our aid. Let those who can and will come with me, but leave the others here."

As you wish.

The cold arms tugged at him. "Come with me, if you want to help," he said. Faithful as always, Castrin stood up first.

"Come on," he said to the others, and several moved to follow.

On the far side of the rock on which Serendola had leaned, another hollow led down to darkness. The wraith's cold hand on his wrist pulled him into a hole through which he had to squeeze; dirt slid along under him, dust rose, making him sneeze and cough, and where the passage went between rocks, he felt every one of his bruises. He heard the others behind him, some muttering loud enough to be heard, though he could not distinguish the words. At last, he fell an arm's length onto a stone floor.

Light brightened around him. He was in a burial chamber floored with scattered and broken bones. Smashed pots and boxes, scraps of fabric, small gleams that might be jewels or coins missed by grave-robbers. In the center, a pile of earth and small stones showed where the roof had been pierced by the attack. The walls were covered with faded pictures of a vanished people, painted on one long side to show rooms in which a feast was being held, and on the other a hunting scene: gaily-dressed men and women on horseback, riding in a forest. The short ends of the chamber contained panels of writing Serendola could not read; a script he had not seen before.

I was old when I died, in a time of peace, and my life-friends died with me at their own will. We and our mounts rested here amid beauty until the Great Time. But we cannot rise then at the gods' call if our bones are scattered.

Serendola and the others looked at the bones. "How many of you?" he asked. "If all the chambers were desecrated, we cannot…"

I and my eight companions, and nine horses. One of us will assist you in discerning which bones belong together, and I must return to ward your companions from the enemy.

"You are the king who died? May I have your name?"

I am, but I have no name in this time. You—you carry your king's blood, do you not?

"I am not a prince," Serendola said. He would neither claim nor deny the king's blood but told what truth he could.

We shall see. With that, the wraith vanished, and one he had not noticed, stouter of build, came from the wall.

In that peculiar light, the work began. Serendola could not have told, of his own knowledge, which fragment of bone went with another to form a whole bone. The wraith directed without words. As they gradually assembled bone after bone, the wraith touched the fragments, and they became whole once more. Then it was putting bone to bone for each individual so all matched. Serendola had never paid much attention to bones in this way; it was wrong to handle them, in his own people's thinking, but it had to be done.

Underground, they had no sense of time passing, and became no more hungry or thirsty than they had been before. They had to dig through the pile of dirt and small stones a handful at a time, picking out each bone fragment, each tooth, and setting them in place, then letting the wraith make them whole. Serendola did not notice when the pile of dirt diminished… when the first small stone lifted from the floor and joined the cracked and shattered stones still out of reach overhead. He noticed as more and more rose that way, as they seemed to melt finally into a painted sky.

One by one they laid the skeletons in place as the wraith directed. The king in the center, the Eight—four men and four women—on his right hand, each with the left hand raised to the shoulder of the one in front. The king's horse's skeleton at his feet, the eight horses of the others on his left hand, all facing the same way, all with the right forefoot raised. Overhead, the chamber's ceiling arched unbroken, the vault bright with shades of blue from pale at one end, with a glittering gold sun just showing to the deep blue-purple of midnight at the other, with bright jewels set as stars.

Even as it was done, the chamber was plunged into darkness, and Serendola heard the grinding of great stones scraping together. Someone's warm hand grasped his; he clasped it. He had understood from the beginning they might die underground. The noise went on for a time he could not measure, even by breaths, and then a dim grey-blue light shaped a doorway. The wraiths came in, all of them, and went to stand one by each skeleton. Last came the king.

You have done well. We honor you. We mourn your dead as our own.

Menis's body floated into the chamber, as if on a pallet, then came to rest on the floor alongside the others.

If you will, we would have him here with us. We have his memories as well as our own.

Serendola knelt beside the body and laid his hand on Menis's brow, then bent and kissed him on the brow and on the lips. "Later," he whispered.

He looked at the wraith-king.

"The others?"

Await above. Your enemy is vanquished; his wealth is yours. But we allow none to settle here again, though for the service you have done, you may remain for a time. Or…

A long pause. Serendola looked at those who had come down with him. It was silent there, a deep, deep silence. *Or as you hold one another as close as we did, you may join us.*

"I am not a king," Serendola said. "And none are so sworn to me."

It is not the oath but the heart. Should one not wish so, he cannot be compelled.

Serendola looked at Menis again, at the ruin of that once-beautiful face, that once-powerful body. In childhood, he and Menis and Agkert had sworn to live and die together. They had cut their thumbs to make their blood and fates one. And so a prince and a prince's bastard cousin and a prince's bastard half-brother had believed in what was not possible, for those who governed them had all said so. Yet there they had come at last to the same decision they had made as stripling boys.

"I must ask the others," Serendola said, looking the wraith-king in the face. "They have the right."

All the wraiths bowed. *They have the right. Go, take your rest and taste the food and wine your enemies left. Taste life, and decide where your heart lies. But should you choose the Long Sleep together, here is the herb you should eat.*

And the wraith-king held out a sprig of it. *It brings death with no pain.*

Serendola led those who had helped in the work up a long, stone-lined passage to the daylight outside. They came out on the side of the mound facing the mountains, and then had to climb back up to where the others were. On the way, Serendola saw many plants of the death herb. They found their companions surrounded by bags of food and jugs of wine, for the wraiths, they said, had moved these things from the enemy's camp for their comfort.

"Not just the nine we saw," Soldin said. He had stayed with Agkert. "Twenty wraith-kings at least, maybe more, each with his eight companions, rose from other tombs under the mound along its length, all glowing like the first, and they cried out in strong voices as they rode through the air, down on the Emperor's troops. We could not see what they did, but we heard the screams… then silence. Then the wraiths came back, bringing us food and drink, and returned below."

"After that," Algon said, "we were stronger, and some of us went to see. The wraiths left all behind: horses, tents, weapons, but no trace of men, alive or dead. We could not leave, for you were below, but we called out to those who had fled alone. All but one returned." He looked rested, and his cheeks had a healthy color.

"Agkert?" Serendola asked.

"Asleep now," Soldin said. "He grieves, but says he knows Menis could not have lived."

Serendola and the others who had been below ate and drank, then told the rest what they had done and seen. In the heat of afternoon, they fell asleep and woke at first-dawn the next morning.

"We have a choice," Serendola told them. "Our pursuers were but one of the Emperor's armies. You are all bravest of the brave, but we are few, and Fuarr has fallen. We cannot gain it back. We can go on, into those mountains, and make a new home perhaps. The wraiths have given us leave to stay here for a brief time, but we cannot stay forever, not as living men. They offer us a peaceful death and a Long Sleep with them, if we will."

A red streak brightened in the east; Serendola turned to it. For the first time in many days, he could sing the sun up in the proper way, and he did so, as if it were his last sunrise. And so it might be, but his hand did not shake when he poured the wine on the stone, and his voice rose steady and strong to the brightening sky. Then he turned back to the others.

"I am not a king, and you have not sworn your death with mine: what will you?"

They talked off and on through the day. Serendola said the least, for he needed to hear more than he needed to persuade, even if he had known for certain what he would persuade them to. He walked across to the enemy camp with several others and saddled and mounted a horse.

He rode around the entire mound, a matter of several sunhands even at a good pace. The sun warmed his shoulders and his back; the horse's movement lifted his mood. This was a good place, a peaceful place; if the wraiths had offered a home there, he would have been willing to set a shovel to the land and farm... but they had not.

And somewhere, he knew, the Sandlord was moving, bringing the desert closer, pushing those who had once lived on the fertile plains to look for new land.

It had begun generations before, and finally the flight from the Sandlord had reached Fuarr, and Fuarr—though now in the hands of the Emperor—would someday be parched and dry, just like the rest. Those stricken by the Sandlord would try to escape, and come there, when they fled Fuarr.

What then would the wraiths do? Kill them all?

When he got back to the little camp on the mound, Agkert motioned him over.

"I know I might live, but... to be honest. I see no hope for me, as I am. For any of us, but particularly me. I will never be whole again." He lifted the stump of his right arm. "To lie with Menis in the Long Sleep would give me ease. Will you forgive me?"

"By the blood we share, there is nothing to forgive. I have thought—"

"No." Agkert reached out with his other arm. "Not you, Serendola! We swore a boy's oath; we are men now. You are the last of Teriond's blood. You must live. You must sire sons. And some of these others do not want to die and be buried here. They will not tell you so, but they want you to live, to lead them away."

His heart sank, heavy as the heaviest stone. "I have no heart for vengeance," he said. "And the Sandlord will come."

"Not in your lifetime. And I am not speaking of vengeance but living. Be their king, Seren. Give them something to live for. And when your sons are grown, and you are near death, come back here if you will. Menis and I will await you. I will see the wraiths let you in. Do this, brother of my blood, for us and for your father."

Agkert's expression changed. "I hear him, the wraith-king," he said. "Hold me close, brother. Let me taste your breath, then let me go."

Serendola bent his head and kissed Agkert as he had Menis, and cradled him until the last breath, then let the wraiths take his body below.

"Will you also go?" asked Castrin. The others watched, their expressions somber.

"No," Serendola said. "I choose life, as long as it lasts, but I hope to lie here when it ends."

Castrin took a deep breath.

"Then we are to see another dawn? And you will be a king to us, as your father was?"

"Many dawns, I hope," Serendola said. "And as you want a king, so I shall be one."

* * *

As his strength and theirs returned, they packed what they could use from the enemy's camp, and rode away on the enemy's horses. In time, they came to a far shore in another realm, and all found ways to live, and some found wives, including Serendola. She bore him three sons, and he taught them, and then other children in that place, where again he was asked to rule. But when his youngest son was old enough, he went to Castrin and put the question to him: *Is it time?*

Castrin nodded, smiling. "I want to go now, before I am too old to travel so far." So, Serendola and Castrin made their way back to the valley coming to it in the morning, with the sun casting shadows before them. By noon, they had found the place they remembered.

Serendola found and plucked leaves of the death herb; they climbed the mound together, and together they ate of the herb.

And no one has yet disturbed their bones.

AUTHOR'S NOTE ON "MY PRINCESS"

Plain daughter of an unloved queen, with two younger, more beautiful sisters born of the next queen, what else is there for her but weapons and war? Certainly not a conventional happy ending, but perhaps a wise choice. The setting is Old Aare, but in a cooler climate, in mountainous terrain. Why is it told from the point of view of the servant/soldier who kept her gear in order? Because he demanded the honor and she didn't want to talk about it. There was more to this story, but it was mostly a depressing political tale of treachery and spite and incompetence. She had plans beyond escape but not the resources to carry them out. I wrote part of it and put it away. No conventional happy endings in any version.

Publication Note: Originally published in *Warrior Princesses,* ed. Elizabeth Ann Scarborough & Martin H. Greenberg, DAW Books, 1998.

My Princess

The princesses in fairy tales are so young and beautiful—or, if plain, gifted with unusual virtues that bring them love and the admiration of their people. The princesses in fairy tales die young, tragically, or live happily ever after, with or without a prince. In those tales (more folk than fairy) of warrior princesses, these are also young, beautiful, brave… the poignancy of putting such rare, fragile beauty in mortal peril is part of the charm.

In reality, the warrior princesses are unlikely to be beautiful or more fragile than the average of mortal flesh, and when they die in battle, no one weeps over the tragedy in terms of roses lost to untimely frost, or delicate crystal shattered by ruinous barbarians. Not for them the wails and tears, the spontaneous outburst of songs; not for them the flowers piled against a palace wall.

I was thinking of this while cleaning my princess's tack, using an old toothtwig on the clotted blood and sweat. Her sister, the Rose of the Kingdom, or her other sister, the Lily of the Morning, neither one of those could walk down the street without a murmur of adoration. They wear the royal clothes well, those two, and smile at everyone, reaching out with gentle hands to touch the shining heads of children, the grey curls of grandmothers. They are beloved, with reason. If they should die before their time—a stupid expression, that, because the time to die is when you die—songs will be sung for them, and enough tears shed to float the bier to some enchanted island.

Her Highness, my princess—though, in truth, they are all my princesses, I claim her especially—would likely die in this war, despite her skill. She would have a funeral, of course, when it was convenient, and her mother would commission a bard to write her a song, and crowds would gather (would be gathered, if necessary, by the household guard) to line the processional way. But her touch is iron and steel; her comfort remote to those she protects. She is not beloved, who strides along with a ring of bootheels, whose very glance is dangerous, out of a face plain and tanned as the flap of a saddle.

I finished the bridle and hung it on a peg. In parades, her parade horse wears the fancy bridle and saddle with the royal arms set onto every possible location. It's not my job to polish that; the royal stables have an entire staff to care for the royal tack, keeping gold and silver and ruby enamel bright. My job is, like my princess's, less showy and more dangerous. It is my job to see that the gear her warhorse wears is whole and sound in every part.

I have been doing this for eight years now. She was a tense, awkward youngster when she came to us, and I was assigned to her—to her horse, actually, though to me it is the same thing. She rode old Ponder then, who had been her father's warhorse—steady, reliable, and—though she did not know this, as indeed neither did her father—voice-trained by the troop commander so that if she should stray into an excess of peril, the horse would bring her home.

We never had to use the command, though. From the first, she showed herself steadier in danger than before it—unusual for any, and especially for princesses. In that first battle—a skirmish, really—she was white to the lips but did exactly what she had been told, unlike her cousin who, eager for glory, spurred his horse into a deep bog and had to be rescued at the cost of fourteen lives.

Now she fights as well as any other eight-year veteran, and her eyes have that look which only veterans acquire, and which nothing but a long peace can take away. Fate has not granted us a long peace—or much peace at all—since my princess was twelve years old and first learning to toss the lance. She does not command all our armies, but she has earned command of some few squadrons of cavalry. Where she commands, the enemy has never raided unscathed; her vigilance has held them at bay even when others slackened their guard.

"Mol—" Her Highness called me. I tucked the rag I was using into the sack that held a lump of saddle soap, twisted the toothtwig into the thong, and went to her.

"Milady." She does not like formal address on the field, and though we have all been ordered by His Grace the noble Duke to address her so, when he is not there we do as she wishes... or somewhat closer to it, since she would prefer to be called Captain only.

"I thought I felt the saddle shift a bit today—would you check with the saddler about restuffing?"

"At once, milady." I glanced up at her face. Five days before, I'd been in the capital, where her sisters had greeted me as they ought... her sisters with the flower-faces, the shining hair, the smiles and graces that everyone associates with princesses. My princess looked more like a queen in exile, weatherworn and dangerous. The word princess fit her as ill as a ball gown would, these last years.

I took the saddle to the saddler, who hummed over it and gave me a sharp glance, as if he suspected me of pilfering wool from its panels. Then he waved me away, and I went back to my work. The bridle done, and I had checked the stitching of the reins. The breastplate, the girths, the crupper and breeching on which the barding hung. While old Festus had the saddle, I could get at the rest of the harness, and by the time I was done, afternoon had dimmed into evening. Beyond the torchlight, I could see nothing. I cleaned my hands carefully and went out of the tent to find that Festus had set the saddle on the stand outside. I moved it under cover and checked every stitch. Then I took saddle and harness to the horse tent where Warning's groom was rubbing the last of the day's mud out of the grey horse's hairy fetlocks with handfuls of dry straw. Festus would have checked the fit, but I was the one who had to be sure every strap of the harness fit.

Warning snuffled at me, hoping for a tidbit, but the groom scolded him. Grooms are jealous, always convinced that the horses they care for become somehow their own. I suppose it's natural, but I have no affection for the tack that is my care—only for the princess whose life it may save. Or not.

Festus had done his usual good work; the restuffed saddle fit Warning's back perfectly. I unrolled the rest of the harness and tried it on. This would have to come down a hole, but—I considered—as the new stuffing compressed, it might need to be shortened again. I made a knot of horsehair, to remind myself to tell Her Highness that in the morning.

Then I set everything ready for tacking up, and went to get my supper. I've heard men complain about the food, but I carry as much flesh as ever, and can stay the march with younger men. War is not for delicate feeders. I took my hunk of ill-baked bread, my bowl of soup more full of cabbage and onion than I like, and squatted near the fire. It was coming on to autumn again; up here in the hills, the night air could be cold. Long habit let me notice how the sentries were placed and how alert they were—good enough, this cold night. I relaxed a bit and ate my supper. She would eat in her tent with her officers around her, and long after I fell asleep in a pile of straw, she would be awake planning for the morrow.

It had been so for almost eight years. I went to sleep expecting it to be so for the next eight, unless she were killed in battle, which was likely enough. That prospect disturbed me; I would be assigned to her flightier cousin, no doubt, and despite my deep respect for the entire royal family, I could not like that scatterbrain.

To bed at war, I wakened to peace—or so the heralds declared, riding into camp in the black belly of night with torches flaring and trumpets sounding. We all roused, thinking at first it was an attack. I had Warning half-saddled when the message got through to me. Peace. A treaty with our old enemies sealed by the marriage of my princess's sisters to the sons of their royal houses—traditional. It would not last; we all knew that. But for now—at least until after the wedding and bedding and birthing of heirs—we would have peace.

I pulled the war saddle off Warning and waited, uncertain whether she would ride back to the capital tonight. Usually she told me herself which tack to use, but this night word came by her bodyservant. She would ride Sudden, not Warning, for his speed; she wanted the lighter gear; she would leave at dawn. I checked that tack, and lay down again for the brief time left me. I could not sleep. Uneasy in my mind, I wondered why, when the peace that we had all desired had come at last.

By the first light, I had Sudden tacked and warmed up for her; unlike Warning, the chestnut has a cold back and needs to be settled or he'll buck on mounting. After getting the kinks out of him, I laid the wool horse-cloak over his back and walked him up and down outside her tent until she was ready. It is not my fault that I heard the voices, for I was where I should have been, following the orders I had been given.

"No," my princess said. I had heard her say no to many things before, but this had an intensity beyond the usual, beyond *No, we'll attack through this gap* or *No, I'm not tired.*

Rumble, rumble, the deep voice of a man whose natural register was even lower than mine.

"But Your Highness must understand the importance of this treaty," said another, more tenor than bass.

"It's different for my sisters," my princess said. I stumbled over air, jerking Sudden's lead, and the horse threw up his head. I soothed him and walked on, but closer to the tent walls. That much is my fault, if you want to apportion fault. "I cannot—" my princess said, her voice going rough as it did when she held the dying, her throat closing against sobs. "I gave all that up—He can't ask now—" They have betrothed her, I thought, though I could hardly believe it; no one trains a falcon and then cages it like a songbird and expects sweet music.

"You will become used to it," said the tenor voice. "It is your duty."

"My duty," she said, "is to my troops and my country."

"You have the order reversed," the deep voice said. It was almost familiar, that voice; I would know it in a moment, or if it spoke louder. "Your duty is to your sovereign, who represents your country. Your duty to your troops ends when you are relieved of command."

I almost snorted, letting out a tiny huff of air that Sudden heard and danced to. I quieted him again. Before she answered, I knew her answer, and it came.

"My duty to my troops will never end," she said, her voice ringing out now in the cold still air. "Their bodies have stood between me—between all of us—and the enemy these eight years."

"Well, in a ceremonial sense, of course, that's true," said the tenor voice. "But your immediate duty—"

"Is to return and obey your sovereign's command," the bass voice finished.

I glanced around. A remarkable number of soldiers had found it necessary to do their morning chores within earshot, though I was closest, having the best excuse. I locked eyes with the color sergeant; his mouth tightened.

"And I am here," the deep voice said. "And my son—"

His Grace, the noble Duke that's who that was, and his son was a lordling only one year older than my princess, with half her experience and the reputation for being just a little slow to engage the enemy. At one time gossip had linked their names, but we could not imagine our princess wedded to such a man, and nothing came of it.

Her voice was tight with anger when she spoke again. "And your son is to command these troops?"

"Yes, Your Highness," said the tenor voice. I glanced at the sergeant again. His face might have been carved out of grey stone in that early light. I saw someone move between the tents, away from hers, and knew the word would pass. The tenor voice went on, when it would have been better silent. "This commission was given by your gracious mother herself. I will endeavor to live up to your example."

Oho. So the tenor was the son we'd heard of. They must have come while I rested, in the deep night; had I dozed, not to hear them?

"It may seem strange at first," the duke said, in a tone he probably meant to be soothing and fatherly, though I knew it would rasp the princess's nerves. "But you will be relieved of this unnatural strain, this hardship, this danger. In peace and safety you will regain your—" He paused. I could have laughed, almost, as he realized the corner into which he'd maneuvered himself. Whatever he said now would be wrong, would insult her—regain youth, beauty, charm? Were these not part of the definition of princess, whether a live princess displayed them or not? "Your peace," he said finally.

"Peace." Her voice rasped on the word, steel on stone. I dared to lead Sudden past the opening to her tent and glance in past the sentries. In the lamplight, she still looked like what she was, and the duke looked like what he was, all courtier. "And you trust this peace, my lord? You trust this peace so much?"

The men's voices dropped again, and I could not hear their words clearly. I could guess much, but I had no proof. And then she came out, pulling her gloves on, her face as still as on any other morning. I held the stirrup for her to mount; she looked down at my face, a long look. "Thank you, Mol," she said. Then, to the duke and his son, who had followed her out. "I want Mol to come with me, for the changes of horse."

"I will need him," the duke's son said. "To see to my tack."

My princess looked at me again, and something flickered behind her eyes. Not fear—I had seen her afraid, in those first years, enough to know what her fear looked like—but something related to it. Wariness, perhaps. Calculation. "Take care of Warning," she said. "Very good care." Then she gathered her reins, and with the escort behind her spurred to a gallop on the way back to the capital.

The duke stayed to breakfast and the midday meal, making sure that everyone knew his son was in command. Then he rode away with his entourage, off to the northeast. The duke's son was not ill-looking, but I did not like the way he ordered me to saddle Warning, or the way he threw the reins to me when he dismounted after exercising the horse. He had a taste for formality; though it was normal for a new commander to hold an inspection, he went at it as though he expected to find some serious problems the enemy had not noticed. Eight years, I thought to myself, and he thinks we're still green?

The duke's son had brought his own warhorse, a roan stallion, but continued to use Warning daily. He rode well enough, with dash I would say, but sat more on his left hip than his right; his horse's saddle showed the characteristic flattening. When I took it to Festus to be restuffed, the duke's son reproved me. I had not asked permission. I ducked my head and apologized, glancing aside at the miniature he had put on his desk in her—his—tent. He had married a sweet-faced girl, if that picture had much likeness, a girl who probably thought he was handsome. I suppose he was—I tried to be fair, but I could feel, as any veteran would, the slow unraveling of the troops, the loosening of strands our princess had knit tight. We obeyed, but day by day obedience became more form than spirit. We said nothing to each other—what was there for soldiers to say about this, that lay too deep for words?—but I met more and more in other eyes the mood I felt behind my own.

The first flurries of snow blew down from the higher hills, and the duke's son ordered a retreat to the lowlands, only a day's march from the capital. He did not leave behind the pickets she would have; he trusted the wedding truce. I heard that some of the captains argued, to no avail. I said nothing; no one would listen if I spoke.

Some days later, we moved even closer to the capital. As an honor to my princess, some of the troops she commanded would be paraded at her wedding. We knew now who she would wed. Not a king's son, after all, but a noble's son from the kingdom to the east. That kind had no unmarried sons; she would marry a cousin.

I could not imagine it, my princess in a wedding gown, pledging herself to a man who by all accounts had never taken the field.

In the city there was no escape from rumor. Her sister princesses were seen daily, at one celebration after another, even walking through the market scattering alms. Their cheeks were rosy in the chill air; they moved as gracefully as reeds in the wind. *She* had not been seen since her return. Locked up, some said, to force her submission. Secluded while serving women did what they could to repair the ravages of eight years in the field. It would take years, a woman in the marketplace said in my presence, to reshape her figure, bleach her complexion, and teach her womanly skills and graces.

I thought of the spears and swords her skill had turned aside, her grace in the saddle. I wanted to hit the woman, but she was a commoner, a cheesemaker by her apron, and she had but said what many thought. They did not think how she had served them, in heat and cold and danger, those eight years—they only compared her to her pretty sisters.

We saw the bridegrooms-to-be, as well. Two were princes of the blood, from the enemies of our west and south: one a slim light-haired fellow scarce taller than I, with a sweet but dangerous twist to his mouth, whose cool blue gaze lingered too long for my taste on the details of the city's walls and gates. And a brown-haired man, somewhat stocky but not fat, who moved like a soldier when he walked and had a scarred left hand. Rumor had it he had been wounded twice in battle: his personal guard bragged in the taverns that he was braver than any. Then there was my princess's bridegroom: stoop-shouldered, with a disgruntled expression that made it clear he thought the others had the best bargain. I saw him smile only when flattered.

The more dangerous rumors were harder to find, but being sure they existed, we searched the more diligently. For what reason was our princess being sacrificed?—for that is what it was. What other purpose had the most noble duke, our commander in chief, for removing her from command of the east, and putting his son there—and then marrying her to that eastern lordling? Those of us most interested spent our last coin on drink and herbs to find out, and the truth we found at last chilled us to the bone. Treachery within treachery... was the whole world rotten but her? She would not live to see a child grown, though she might live to bear a few, if that itself did not kill her. But no more, for her, the open air and fields, not even the joy of the chase.

Finally, and only days before the weddings, I saw my princess again. She came into the stable yard, while I was polishing the duke's son's tack, and I did not recognize her at first. She looked thinner and softer, tricked out in women's clothes; she wore a tight-laced dress and a fur-trimmed cloak, and low boots with pointed toes. Her hair was piled up, with loose tendrils blowing... I realized that most of it was false, since she had not had time to grow out her warrior's crop. Her face looked strange, until I saw that she had been made up to look less brown. In the chill wind outside, her own color splotched through the powder and paint.

She knew me, though, and came near. "Mol," she said.

"Your Highness." In this courtyard, only formality would serve, and I was well aware of those who watched and listened.

"Warning?"

"Is well, Your Highness," I said.

"He rides him?"

I knew the lack of name was intentional. "Yes, Your Highness. But he is not a bad rider."

"That's good." Her eyes shifted away, very unlike her old direct gaze.

"I'm... sorry," I ventured, very low. She looked at me then, a glance as sharp as a dagger; I almost flinched.

"You... know?"

"Yes, Your Highness."

"It won't work," she said, as softly. "He doesn't want me; I don't want him. I can't—it's too late, after all that's—"

A voice called querulously from the doorway. She glanced over her shoulder, the only furtive movement I'd ever seen from her. It was her husband-to-be, hunched against the chill like a vulture. She did not move toward him, but stood erect, tense. He came out, calling her name again.

"You'll be late," he said. "And this wind, my love, will roughen your complexion." He looked at her as men look at ugly women.

I heard her growl, such sound as she had made once when she found one of our men had been mutilated. Not loud, but intense. I glanced his way; he had not heard it.

"What do you do here?" he asked, coming closer. "Who is this fellow?"

"Mol," she said, with no resonance in her voice. "He cared

for my tack in battle. I came to thank him for his care, that preserved my life in those years, and to thank my troops—"

"Surely you need not come yourself," he said, with a chuckle I wanted to push back down his throat. "You have servants now, to carry such messages—"

"And to see my old horse," she said. "Since you say I will not need him—"

"No, indeed," he said, agreeably enough, looking around. "We breed fine horses at home, fit for a lady's pleasure. You shall have a nice mare for your excursions and, when you no longer wish to ride, a matched team for your carriage."

She had stiffened at *no longer wish to ride*; her gaze slid past mine, toward the stable opening. "Warning is here?" she asked me abruptly.

"Yes, Your Highness," I said. I could feel the man's gaze on my bent head. "Left aisle, fifth stall." I almost told her where her war saddle was hung but did not.

"What a name for a lady's horse," the man said. "You will be glad, I'm sure, to ride gentler beasts. But let us go and see your... Warning... one last time. I understand that women are sentimental about such things."

Because I was looking down, I saw the knuckles of her sword hand whiten, the tendons standing out in her wrist. I dared not look up, dared not meet whatever expression she had found to answer him. They walked off. I saw that he was trying to offer his arm, and she was not seeing it... deliberately, that much was clear. From behind they looked as ill-matched a pair as Warning and Sudden in double harness. Her shoulders were still broader than his, despite the weeks she had not practiced; the lady's boots she wore forced her to a shorter stride, but she swung her leg from the hip anyway.

When they came back across the courtyard, she neither looked at me nor spoke, but one of her hands flicked, as if something had stung her. I knew by that she would return.

No one walked the castle grounds at night unchallenged. No women came out after dark at all. I saw with my back propped on a sack of corn, restitching the reins to the roan horse's bridle, and listening to the evening noises. No one walked by night unchallenged, but by day the bustle increased, with more and more wedding guests crammed into the city, with more and more servants crowding the workspaces. Hard to do anything without being observed, but harder yet to keep track of all the newcomers. Eight of us, this evening, were sharing the lamplight in one small alcove, all working on tack. I glanced around. Festus the saddler replacing the saddle flap. Two foreigners, cleaning a tangle of bridles. Three more grooms from the old troop, mending halters and other gear, and one palace flunky soaping a harness. This wasn't the place to clean harnesses—they had a separate shed for that—and he wasn't doing it right, anyway—so I assumed he was watching us. When he left, the harness still half-cleaned, it was clear he'd decided we were harmless.

We were supposed to sleep in the loft, but it was noisy up there—half the grooms snored, I had complained repeatedly—so I slept on the ground floor on a pile of sacking. With the city so full, no one scolded me for this. I lay there, looking out the stable door, listening to the horses shift and stamp or make water. So it was I saw the kitchen boy edging along the wall before dawn, a shadow against the torches across the courtyard.

"Mol," came the soft voice.

"Um." I swallowed the natural thing to say; here it would be fatal.

"I...cannot marry him. I must get away." She sounded apologetic; they had shamed her, who had never turned away from danger before.

"I know," I murmured into her ear. I nearly choked on the scent they made her wear, like a tavern wench's. If the guards got close enough they'd know she was no kitchen boy. I told her the little I could, and sent her back in only a few minutes. We could not get past the gates at night, or against arms. Yet Festus and the color sergeant and I had an idea which might work—or at least might give her a better death then the one she faced in that dull lordling's birthing chamber. She nodded, when I'd finished, and pressed my arm with a hand still strong enough to hurt.

The duke's son had planned to ride his own roan stallion at the head of the troops, but the stallion came up lame that morning. The duke's son bit his lip, annoyed, and told me to saddle Warning. He did not like her saddle, but he had not told me to have another stuffed to fit Warning's back. I took her war saddle off the rack, and checked it over a last time. Strap by strap and buckle by buckle, I fastened the harness and gear onto the grey horse. Into the saddlebags I put the required supplies, knowing the sergeant would inspect them. The duke's son mounted, narrowly missing my head with his boot as he swung his leg over while I held the stirrup. "I wish this horse fit my saddle," he said irritably. "I'll have to get a new one."

He would indeed. I ran a cloth over his boots with extra care.

After he rode off, I knelt in the roan stallion's stall and pulled out the hair I'd run through the horse's front leg, through the space between bone and tendon. I hoped he would recover quickly. Then I mounted and rode out to join the troop. At least they had let her name the men she wanted to have parade before the crowd. All, except the duke's son, were ready.

The crowds cheered her sisters, their breath steaming in the cold air. In their furred hoods, her sisters looked indeed like the flowers they had been called. She, in her carriage, looked nothing like them; the crowd's cheers were perfunctory for her, and louder for her escort. I rode beside the carriage horses, eyeing the postilions on the nearside of each pair. They rode well enough, but not like cavalrymen—and they would not expect what was coming.

We were just turning into the market square when I saw Warning flinch. The duke's son's heavy hip had done its work, pressing hard enough to force the sharp flint through the cloth sack Festus had made for the saddle panel. We had argued, Festus and I, over how much padding to put in; the horse must not buck on mounting, but must feel the stone before the procession ended. The duke's son sat deeper, and Warning flinched again. I hated doing this to a horse but—we had to unseat the duke's son without actually touching him. We needed that confusion. I glanced again at the postilions and let the fingers of my right hand, held down at my side, flick twice. I did not look at my princess. She was not an eight-year veteran for nothing.

The next turn was to the left, around the square, and I knew the duke's son would slip to his inside hip; he always did. Warning flinched, then hopped; the duke's son, as I expected, yanked on the reins and sat back heavily, clenching his legs. Warning whirled and half-reared. Behind him, the color sergeant said, "Warning—look out, sir!" and Warning went straight up and came down bucking. The duke's son stayed on for two bucks— one more than I had bet; I'd lost three silver pence on that— and then rolled off. The color sergeant cut Warning off neatly in front, but his wild grab at the reins went carefully astray.

"Warning!" My princess called, in her old voice, and the grey horse broke into a canter toward us, kicking out when anyone tried to grab the loose reins. I whirled my own mount, spurred, and he kicked the lead carriage horse and postilion square on. As Warning came by, I slid off, all apologies, and ran to him. A hand under the near side of the saddle, and the pesky flint in its bag came away, into the front of my uniform. I held reins and stirrup while the princess lunged from the carriage onto his back, skirts all a-tumble. Warning steadied, without the flint gouging his back; my companions, meanwhile, had dismounted all the postilions, and cut the traces of the carriage horses, who fled plunging into the crowd.

Faster than it takes to tell it, we were charging past the rear of the procession, the crowd scattering. Our princess slashed at her skirts with the dagger I handed her, and by the time we cleared the gates, she was a ridiculous figure indeed, with a ruff of skirt and underskirt about her waist and torn white silk hosen on her muscular legs, the beribboned sleeves of her wedding gown blowing, her wig hanging by one remaining ribbon. She yanked it off her head and threw it away, grimacing as a lock of her own hair came with it.

Beyond the gate we vanished, people said later, but sixty armed men and a warrior princess don't vanish. She had more respect among the farmers whose land she'd protected all those years, where she'd insisted we could not take even a stray chicken for dinner without asking. So we made it to the forest, and before she was quite frozen, she had changed into the clothes we'd brought for her. I don't think any of us, man or woman, veteran or novice, thought for a moment of those glimpses of her body we'd seen then.

* * *

My princess died far away from court and crowds; the only flowers on her grave are those wildings that seeded there from the bunches I laid on it. You would ask, I know, of what she died, and when, and the number of her wounds. You would ask if she ever married, if she had children, if she lived to old age. You would like to know how her sisters fared, how her own land survived, if it did. You would make a tale, perhaps, of the gallant swordswoman, or the poor misguided girl, or the wild adventurer. But I tell no more than this: her death, like her life, won my respect, and I do not give that easily.

AUTHOR'S NOTE ON "THE SHEPHERD'S TALE"

More legend than story. Dort—the Master Shepherd's name—showed up in the first Paks book as part of her name, "Dorthansdotter." In the early days of writing in Paksworld, many such personages showed up, interacted with "younglings" of their trade or craft, and played tricks on them to see which deserved to be... whatever it was. Does a "brickyard boy" aim too high? Maybe someday I'll have a story of Master Bricklayer, too. The original story was misplaced when I put "in a safe place" a large group of Paksworld stories that has never shown up again. So, this is a reimagined story but the basics are there, and the details much enhanced by a number of YouTube videos of sheep farming, from several different places with a variety of sheepdogs and livestock-guardian dogs. Thanks due to all and their brilliant dogs.

Publication Note: "The Shepherd's Tale" is new, written exclusively for *Deeds of Wisdom*.

THE SHEPHERD'S TALE

Tab came away from the baker's stall and headed across the market square, angry and hopeless. His lord's factor had disputed his right to sell a lame, footsore ewe that could not keep up with the herd.

It was his lord's sheep, the factor insisted; his lord should get the payment. Tab deserved only the minimal fee for bringing the sheep to market. The judicar agreed.

And for those two coppers, the baker said, he could have only a pair of two-day-old loaves, hard and dry now. Not nearly enough to feed his family.

Across the square he could hear a storyteller's clear, musical voice.

Tab edged around the crowd, trying to hear without being obvious. The name "Dort" caught his attention. He knew part of that tale.

Dort, the Master Shepherd, born of Alyanya, the Lady, Goddess of Peace and Plenty. It was said Dort's father was a cave giant with all-seeing eyes and rams' horns and cloven hooves like sheep.

"—far in the West," the man said, his hands shaping the air into distance, into hills and mountains. "And every one of his sheep—" His fingers wiggled, making a band of sheep almost visible, moving along the slope his other hand suggested. "*Every one*," the storyteller said again, "has a fleece of shining gold, and every golden hair is pure gold, fine as the thread a spider spins, and can be woven into the finest gold cloth." His fingers moved, drawing out the thread of gold, his eyes following the gleam his voice described.

"How do you suppose he found sheep with golden fleece?"

He paused.

Behind the storyteller, a lanky boy stood up, holding a tall hat in his hands. His gaze roamed over the back of the crowd, touched Tab, and moved on. He moved through the crowd, hat held out.

Tab turned away. He couldn't even listen to a story, even part of a story, when he had nothing to give. Before faces followed the coin collector's movements, before anyone noticed him, he had to move on.

Tab could not stop thinking about the old tale, even as he turned into the lane out of the village. If only he could get some of that golden fleece. Not a whole fleece, of course not, but a single small tuft caught in a thornbush would surely—*must*—be valuable enough to feed his family for a while.

He shook his head.

He would never see a gold-fleeced sheep or meet the Master Shepherd. It was probably a lie, anyway. He had never seen gold, himself, but he'd heard about gold: coins, rings, bracelets, were gold. Gold was hard; gold was heavy. Wool couldn't be gold; it was soft and light. So, the stories were all lies, made of air, not gold.

He scowled, hearing jovial voices singing inside a tavern as he passed. Easy for *them* with their full bellies. The smell of fresh-baked bread… and meat… made his belly clench. He strode on, away from the town, back to the fields he didn't own, the sheep he didn't own, the flimsy hut he didn't own, and the wife and children he must somehow save from starvation.

That night, Tab dreamed of a flock of gold-fleeced sheep grazing on a green mountainside, and two sheepdogs, one large, white, and shaggy and one smaller, black-and-white. He was not given to remembering dreams or taking notice of them, but this time he told his wife, when he woke, about both the storyteller and the dream.

"See if you dream it again tonight," his wife said. "If it means anything, it will repeat."

This time, the dream began almost as soon as he closed his eyes, or seemed to. There in the distance, against a pale sky, the loftiest mountains rose, white-tipped and otherwise blue-purple with distance. Only a little nearer, he saw hills almost familiar, for hills came down in the plain only a short distance away. In the dream he walked faster than a man could walk, the land passing under his feet without effort, until he was climbing a hill or mountain not so tall as the others, and at the top, the slope rolled back down into a bowl, and in the bowl the golden sheep grazed, inside a ring of ten large stones. The guardian dogs looked at him and did not bark, for they lay beside a huge man sitting on a boulder—surely, that must be Dort—talking to a large, dark-haired, big-nosed woman on another boulder.

His wife, maybe? Tales about the Master Shepherd had never mentioned one.

In the dream, Tab turned away and looked back toward his home, far away and far below. He woke, and told his wife.

"You should go," she said.

"What will you do?"

"Stay alive until you return. Take the sheep with you when you go, as far as their usual pasture, and I'll tell the factor when he comes you're up in the hills with the flock. Then we'll go watch the sheep. Find Dort and tell him you need a tuft or two of that golden fleece."

"But—"

"I can dig cattails, and the wild grasses are seeding here. I have my grinder." She reminded him of the woman in the dream, black-haired, with a proud nose, and though she was thinner than that woman, he knew she was brave and strong.

So, off Tab went, with half a fist of hard, dry bread and his waterskin, and day by day walked toward the higher hills, until he saw the line of mountains appear on the sky, and the hill that reminded him of his dream rising above the lower hills. He found a few berries the wild things had not eaten, and some seeding grasses, and ate as little of his remaining bread as he could.

Then he came upon a woman in rags lying on the ground beside the trail. She moaned as he came near. He could see her rags were loose on her; she looked starved, old, near death, with thinning white hair, dark eyes blurred with age, her face near fleshless, nose prominent, arms and legs like sticks.

She reminded Tab of his grandmother the day she died.

Tab stopped, looking down at her. "Hungry," she whispered. "Please?"

Tab sat down, opened his sack. He'd only nibbled the half-fist of bread he'd taken, but it was down to a small lump, no bigger than the end of his thumb. "Thank you," she said, snatching it quickly and stuffing it into her mouth. She swallowed, then said "Where are you going?"

"To see the Master Shepherd," Tab said. "My flock is poorly.

"Wouldn't it do more good to take better care of your own

sheep? Who's watching them while you travel?"

"My wife and oldest boy," he said. "And my lord will not let me graze the sheep where I would."

"Well, at least you thought of *that*." She sounded much stronger now but still lay there, unmoving. "Do you have any water?"

"No," he said. His waterskin and his mouth were both dry.

"There's a spring over there…" Her bony finger gestured to the side of the hill. "I am thirsty too."

She annoyed him; she'd eaten all his bread, and now gave him advice and orders like the old women in the village who'd scolded him after his father died. But he stood, feeling the ache in his hips and knees, and went around the slope. He found the spring at last, farther away than he'd expected, drank several mouthfuls, filled his waterskin and brought it back to her. She lay where he'd left her. Her eyes seemed a bit brighter, perhaps from the bread, and, when she had drunk half a waterskin, brighter still.

"Thank you," she said then. "So, you want to meet the Master Shepherd? Then you must do as I tell you. From here, you must look ahead. What do you see?"

"A stony path up this hill; I can see the mountains far ahead."

"Good. Now close your eyes and think of that path you're on… is it aimed straight?"

"Yes…"

"You must understand," she said, "that the Master Shepherd is not found on the hills we know but on the hills the Elders wandered when the world began. And he is an Elder, a son of Alyanya herself. To find him, you must tread the path he trod. Keep your eyes closed, night and day, to keep your sight of the right path clear. Open your hand to me."

He opened his hand and felt her old hand grasp it… was she standing?… and nearly opened his eyes to look, but she pushed a wad of what felt like cloth into his hand and folded his hand closed while speaking. "No… do not open your eyes. Wrap this cloth around your head over your eyes. Walk the path your inner sight shows you. Walk with courage… go!" The last word felt like a blow on his back, driving him away.

He took a step, then another. With his eyed closed, the cloth snug to his head, he could still see, narrow and bright, the path with its stones. He was ten steps away before he realized he did not have his stick, and nearly stumbled, but forced himself to go on. He was almost sure this would not work, but step after step, faster and faster, far hills came nearer. The air felt fresher, cooler, scented with herbs he had never smelled before, and then, from a distance, he smelled sheep.

Tab's view of the path was so narrow that he missed a sudden turn at the top of a slope, tripped, and fell into a thorn bush, landing hard enough to knock the breath from him. When he could, he pushed the cloth from his eyes and was face to face with a tuft of golden wool caught in the same thorns that scratched his arms. Carefully, he backed out of the bush and reached for the tuft of wool. It felt both heavier and silkier than a tuft that size from his own sheep, and the sunlight glinted yellow on it.

There it was in his hand, the treasure he had come for. The old woman had told the truth. He raised his head and looked around. Before him, the slope dropped away, more steeply than his dream had shown, the path zigzagging down into a wide bowl with ten stone pillars forming a circle in the bottom.

In the center of that circle, a pool of water reflected the sky.

Along the sides of the bowl gold-fleeced sheep grazed, ewes with their lambs on the slope directly below, a smaller flock of rams in the distance.

Tab tucked the tuft of wool into the bight of his kilt, then backed away from the bush on hands and knees. He didn't see the dogs of his dream, or Dort, or the woman. No need to talk to Dort, with that handful of gold fleece in his kilt, he thought. Maybe just stay low, and—

He jerked upright as a huge hand grabbed the back of his neck and yanked him up until only the toes of his sandals scuffed the ground. He couldn't even breathe.

"THIEF!" came a roar from overhead. Now he saw dogs, the white and the piebald, one to either side, mouths open snarling, showing teeth like knives, ears and tails up. "Another damned human thief, after my sheep! I thought so! That's what troubled the ground these past days, mortal feet on immortal hills!"

"Let him breathe," said another voice, neither as loud nor as angry but by no means weak.

The grip on his neck released, replaced by a solid tug on his hair, as if he might try to run. He landed hard on his feet. The hand turned his head as a man might an apple, thumb against his ear.

Tab gasped in one breath, another. Now he could see what held him, a giant, dressed as he himself was, in shepherd's kilt and long cloak, a leather sling tied around his head to hold back his hair, sandals. The giant—it must be Dort himself—held a great shepherd's crook in his other hand.

"Why should I not smash him with my crook?" the giant asked, leaning down to look Tab in the face. "He's a thief. Come to steal my flock, my precious lambkins."

"I don't think so," said the other voice.

Tab looked, and saw the woman from his dream. Black hair, black eyes, a strong but plain big-nosed face. "He looks hungry to me."

"He looks starved as a wolf," the giant said. He let go of Tab's head. "Do not run," he said, "or my dogs will tear you."

"I won't run," Tab said, surprising himself with the firmness of his voice. So, this was Dort, much bigger than he had realized. As were his dogs, and probably his sheep.

But his knees still shook. Hunger and thirst both, he thought to himself as he realized he was falling. Stones bruised his knees. His cheek lay on the dirt. He had traveled all that way... and now he would die, and then his wife and children... He felt no fear but great sorrow for the uselessness of his quest.

"What's wrong with him?" Dort asked.

"I told you," the woman said. "Hunger, thirst, exhaustion. And whatever drove him to that effort. I don't think he's a thief."

"What do you think, then?" Dort asked. Tab, on the ground, closed his eyes as the white dog came nearer, growling. "If not a thief, why did he take that tuft of my wool and start to creep away, Torre?"

"A poor shepherd come to beg your help," she said. "Happen he has a tale to tell—"

"A tale of lies," Dort said. "They mostly do, thieves. Excuses. A sick wife, a hungry child, a debt they cannot pay."

"You saw him come over the rim," she said. "Eyes closed and bound: those who come that way have passed the first test on the way, you know."

"Even you can err, Torre."

On that second hearing, Tab recognized the name: Torre.

Torre Bignose?

Torre of the Necklace?

That Torre? A legend as much as Dort. She did fit the description: why had he not thought of her before? And the old woman... was she also Torre? On that thought, awareness rolled away into a black cloud, of her hair or of night itself, he could not have said.

He woke wrapped in something warm, leaning against something alive. It moved, and soft fur touched his neck, then a large, smooth, wet tongue licked his face. Dog. The big one.

When he blinked, he saw it was almost dark, heard the crackling of a small fire, smelled food, and then recognized a stone pillar rising against the darkening sky.

"He's awake," Torre said. "You'd better give him a drink and then food."

Tab tried to move, but the warmth around him proved to be wrapped tightly; he was swaddled like a baby. Dort picked up the bundle and unwrapped him until he stood. The wrapping had been Dort's great cloak, much larger than his own. "Sit down," Dort said. He sounded perfectly calm. "Not on my dog; on a stone."

Tab looked behind him; the white dog was waist-high, like the stones the others sat on.

Tab sat. The white dog came nearer and leaned against him, warm in the chill air. It was like being leaned on by a pony.

The smaller dog lay by Dort's feet. "Here is water—" Dort offered Tab a waterskin he recognized as his own, now plumply full.

Tab drank cool water as Dort held out a piece of bread torn off a loaf. "Lady's grace," he said. "No exchange."

Tab took it. It tasted nothing like the simple bread shepherds made in camp but like all nourishing foods together: bread, cheese, herbs, meat, even the sweetness of berries.

He had never tasted anything like it.

He made himself eat slowly, as a guest should. Over his head Dort muttered something to the white dog, who moved off through the sheep.

Tab could see better as he ate and realized all the sheep were gathered in a wide circle between the fire and the pond, inside the circle of pillars, as in his dream.

When he had eaten and drunk his fill, Dort turned to him again. "Now you must tell me true, human. Are you indeed a shepherd? And a good one or bad one?"

"I am a shepherd," Tab said. "I have tried to be a good one, but... my flock has not prospered." He thought of all the reasons it had not, including his greedy lord and the scornful senior shepherds, but in this place, and to the Master Shepherd himself, the reasons sounded like excuses. "I have not been good enough," he said, after a long pause. "And I don't know how to do better."

"Who trained you?" Dort asked.

"Nobody. When my father died, the lord of the land told me to be a shepherd."

"Your father wasn't a shepherd?"

"No... he was a bricklayer. The lord had enough bricklayers, he said, and I should be a shepherd."

"Didn't other shepherds—"

"I wasn't a shepherd's son. A brickyard boy."

"What means that?"

"Dirty, smelly—we boys trod manure into the clay to make it hold together with the straw, to make bricks. Stink-foot, they called us."

Many more questions later, about his work with sheep, when the sky had gone completely dark, Dort gave a huge sigh. "I've heard of worse shepherds, but you are not a good shepherd. Yet. Do you want to be a good shepherd?"

"Yes," Tab said. And then, boldly: "Will you teach me?"

"No," Dort said. "I have my own duties, more than just tending this flock here, and it would take too long."

Torre stirred, beside him. "How long?"

"To become a good shepherd? Years, for a beginner. For someone who's learned the wrong things from bad shepherds... more years to unlearn and relearn."

"Are you landbound?" Torre asked Tab.

"Landbound? I don't own any land—"

"Can you leave, go somewhere else, or are folk there bound to the land?"

"Bound to the land's lord," Tab said. "We came into the land with the lords, from far in the south, so my da and grandda said, and we plain folk are bound to them, for life."

"I don't like that," Torre said, with a look at Dort.

"Nor I." Dort's words growled.

"This land should not be smirched with such human conceits. Humans are not Elders to make such rules even for humans."

"But everyone I know is like that," Tab said. "Even merchants have bound apprentices, and everyone working on a farm is bound to the land and lord and whatever craft the lord assigns."

They both looked at him as if he should know better. Tab felt his ears getting hot. It was true. Everyone knew it.

"It's no life for you and yours," Torre said. "That finnik of a landlord—"

"But we have other matters," Dort said. "Listen closely, little man. Your claim on me is that you are a shepherd, and as Master Shepherd, it is my right to test your claim. Do you understand?"

Tab did not, entirely, but knew the right answer and nodded. "Yes, Master Shepherd."

"Then I will make this test for you. You will sleep this night, and tomorrow, when the sun strikes the top of the stones, you will shepherd *my* flock for a complete circuit of the sun, dawn to dawn. I will have that time to rest, as I very rarely do. I know every one of my flock and I will know how well you cared for them the next day. If they suffer injury from your inattention, you will have nothing but punishment from me, now or later, but if you are diligent and gentle, I will help you with more than that tuft of wool you stole."

Tab slept dreamless that night, and woke as the sky brightened. Torre smiled at him in the early light. She had lit a fire, and he smelled bread; Dort lay asleep between his dogs. The sheep were watching him, ears twitching. "You have just time for breakfast before the sun comes over the rim," Torre said. Sure enough, when he had eaten bread and cheese, and tucked more bread into his bag, and drunk his fill of water from the pool, sun touched the tops of the pillars.

Both dogs were awake now. The sheep edged slyly toward the gaps between the pillars of stone, ignoring Tab but clearly aware of the dogs. Dort slept on, snoring loudly enough to wake an echo off the western slope.

Tab realized he had neither staff nor crook, and did not know what commands the dogs understood. Nor did he know the dogs' names. He tried to estimate the flock's size, but all the sheep were moving.

"Lady Torre—"

"Just Torre. I must leave: I have errands."

"Yes, lady… Torre. Do you know the dogs' names? And— would it be all right to borrow the Master Shepherd's crook?"

"Snow and Storm," she said, pointing to the white, then the piebald. "Dort's crook may have powers you don't know how to use." She reached behind the hip high-rocks that reflected heat from the fire. "I'll find you a stick."

Tab approached the white dog first. "Snow?" he said; the dog looked at him and then turned its head away. "Storm?" as he looked at the smaller piebald. Again a quick glance of acknowledgement and then the dog turned away, watching the sheep. At the far margin of the flock, a dozen rams trotted out between the pillars.

"Snow," Tab said, this time sure of the dog's name. "Wayyy!" he said next, louder, and waved his heart-side arm. He had heard other shepherds use *Way* and *Bye* for directions heart-hand or sword-hand to their dogs, which way to start a gather, and *Coo* and *Dun* to follow the sheep or come back to him. He'd taught one puppy himself, only to have it disappear one night. Snow did not seem to know that first command; the dog stood looking from side to side, then back to Tab.

Tab had no idea what commands Dort used; he hoped the dog could learn quickly.

He waved his left arm out and down. "WAY!" Snow moved slowly in the correct direction; Tab called, "Attaboy, good Snow!" and the dog sped up a little as sheep poured through the gaps between pillars.

Tab strode up the slope himself, and glanced around to find that five ewes and two rams had followed him (or the rams had followed the ewes) while the bulk of the sheep were moving directly away. Snow had not circled the herd but walked behind them.

"SNOW!" The dog glanced over its shoulder and paused. "Dun! DUN!" Instead of coming toward him, Snow faced him and sat down.

Tab felt the first trickle of nervous sweat down his back. What if none of the usual commands worked? He couldn't imagine retraining Dort's dogs. "Uh... here, Snow!"

The dog stood up and took a tentative step closer. "Good Snow. Come on..."

Tab was moving already toward the main mass of sheep. Then he saw a black-and-white streak rushing toward them... not a wolf... Storm? Before Tab could get to the sheep, or Snow, Storm had hit the flock like an arrow, splitting it into two panicky groups. Snow leapt toward Storm, barking. Now the sheep erupted in all directions.

Tab yelled again. "Snow, DUN. Storm, DUN." Both dogs dropped where they were, facing him.

That was only the beginning. For the rest of the morning, Tab switched back and forth between trying to teach the dogs the commands *he* knew and trying to urge the sheep into a more-compact group, where he could see all of them, get a count of them, and get them used to him.

The morning seemed as long as some days he'd worked back home.

He never managed a count, never got all the sheep into one snug circle, though he now recognized certain individuals. He'd noticed a lamb limping, managed to catch it and remove a thorn just above its left front hoof. Snow helped in that, blocking its mother away from the frantic lamb as Tab felt along its leg and pulled out the thorn. A different lamb got mired in the pond; he pulled it out. Two ewes managed to get caught in a bramble thicket, and another stumbled and rolled down a slope, to land upside down in one of the many creeks that fed the pond.

He freed all three.

Perhaps as a result of his work, the sheep were less nervous now when he walked among them, and both dogs were at least attentive to his signals, though they their responses varied.

By midday, with the sun high and hot overhead, Tab had, he hoped, convinced Snow and Storm both to go *around* the flock and slowly gather them. Or perhaps the flock had decided on its own to come back to the center for a drink from the pond. That's when he noticed that the Master Shepherd, who had seemed to be still sleeping peacefully long after sunrise, had disappeared, along with his crook.

Tab sat down on one of the rocks near the pond, dipped his headcloth into the water to wipe his face, and discovered it had changed shape and substance. Now it was a sling, a proper sling of dark leather, like Dort's. Well. Did that mean he'd *need* a sling? He still thought he needed a crook.

He gathered some small round stones anyway, tucking them in the bight of his kilt.

He watched a lamb stick its head under a ewe's flank, tail wagging, but the ewe butted it away. Wrong ewe? The lamb tried again; the ewe pulled away. Her bag looked swollen; he leaned down to look closer. A sore teat? He had nothing to put on it; he looked around to see if Dort had left anything between the rocks. There—a stone pot, lidded with a piece of bark. He sniffed the odd-looking stuff inside.

It smelled sharp, herbal, like the leaves his wife had crushed to use on her own breast when the babe had sucked it sore.

He brought the pot with him and—moving carefully—managed to get a grip on the ewe, taking her to the ground and onto her back without a fight. He dabbed two fingers into the pot, holding two of her legs with the other hand, and spread the ointment on her teats. One was more swollen than the other. He let her stand but kept hold of her fleece. She relaxed faster than he expected, and the lamb pushed under his arm, aiming for the less-swollen teat. Could the ointment have worked that fast? The lamb suckled vigorously.

Of course: a demigod's treatments should work faster than his own.

When he went to put the pot back where he'd found it, he saw a length of wood lying in the shadow. How had he missed it before? He drew it out, noting the stub of a limb at its narrower end. Not a real crook, but should work better than a straight stick. He smoothed off the rougher bits with his knife.

The flock moved again, out from the pond, and Tab discovered he'd stiffened again from the morning's work. Well, nothing for it but more work to loosen up again. The afternoon, long and hot, stretched on and on, with more of the various difficulties sheep could get into. He dealt with them as best he could; the improvised crook definitely helped in catching and holding a sheep.

The dogs helped more. As the day waned, he led one group after another back down to the pond until all the sheep had collected inside the circle of pillars. The dogs sat down by him, and he found, between the rocks, a sack of dried meat and bones, and a smaller one of bread and hard cheese. The dogs gnawed at their dinner while he walked through the flock, checking for lameness, any sign of illness.

Darkness rose around them, in that bowl. Stars appeared overhead.

Tab ached all over and yet… he felt pride, too. He had worked harder than ever before, and while he could not claim to be excellent, he had saved a few lives, mended a few hurts. The sheep had seemed so big, so powerful, at first, but now he was not afraid of them. The strange golden glitter in their eyes no longer looked alien.

It was hard to stay awake… so quiet, and he was so tired. He walked around the herd once, twice, three times. He sat down, just for a few minutes… it was so quiet, and the sheep were surely asleep as well. Even Snow was asleep, snoring, and Storm sat quietly. His eyelids sagged, and he slept.

To wake disoriented, with Snow roaring nearby and Storm barking and snarling a distance away.

And the eerie howls of wolves.

Total dark but for a few glowing coals, and much colder; Tab felt the occasional cold sting of a raindrop. The unseen flock surged this way and that, lambs bleating, older sheep baaing and grunting, their hooves making an unsteady rhythm. One gave a cry, almost a scream, he'd never heard before, then the snarling of wolves ripping at it.

Tab grasped his sling and felt in the bight of his kilt for a stone.

He could see nothing in the dark. He stumbled forward, into the remaining coals, and one flared up. As he balanced himself with his staff, desperate not to fall into the coals, the tip of the staff caught fire; he pulled it up and the flare of light showed the eye-glow of wolves advancing all around the flock. He whirled his sling, let the stone fly; that wolf fell. He reached quickly for another one and a spare he put in his mouth. Again and again, the stones flew from his sling, and struck a wolf... most fell and did not rise again. But there were so many, a big pack, and soon he was out of stones he'd already gathered.

He heard another sheep's dying cry.

Tab waved his flaming staff and ran at the remaining wolves, trying to strike them, but they were faster, more agile. They switched from attacking the sheep to attacking him. Snow appeared out of the dark, mouth already bloody from fighting a wolf, and knocked aside one wolf that leapt at Tab.

"Sheep!" Tab said. "Protect them, if I—" A weight hit his back, and jaws clamped on his shoulder; another wolf caught his leg, yanked him off balance. He dropped the staff and fell hard, the breath knocked out of him. For another instant, he could not see or think; the pain in his shoulder… was gone, and a dome of light covered the bowl. He could see sheep, tightly packed. Snow and Storm both, between the sheep and the remaining wolves, now in retreat. He could feel his own hot blood running down his shoulder, his leg, smell the stink of the wolves' breath. He tried to sit up. Strong hands turned him, and then he could see Dort in the midst of the sheep, sending fiery darts after the fleeing wolves. He saw Torre—she was beside him.

"You'll mend," she said, laying a hand on his leg. That pain vanished.

"The flock?" He tried to sit up; she put an arm behind his back to help him. There beside him was his staff, the blackened wood merging into an iron spike, and the top…the top was a perfectly shaped crook with its neck sized to the necks of Dort's sheep. No, it must be Dort's own crook; he must have dropped it when he threw fire at the wolves—and here was Dort, come to demand an accounting, surely.

Dort stood over him, with the dogs crowding his legs, ears back, tails wagging. "Good dogs," Dort said, fondling their ears with one hand. "Good boy, Snow; good, brave Storm." Dort's other hand held his own crook…and beside Tab lay the stick-turned-crook. Tab looked back and forth between the two crooks, bewildered.

"Surely, you have enough," Torre said to Dort.

Enough what? Tab wondered.

"It's not dawn yet," Dort said. He sighed, as if Torre had said something. "All right. It's enough." He looked directly at Tab. "I doubted you. I thought you had no parrion for sheep but were just a bumbler of a shepherd. Born a brickyard boy, as you said. But Torre convinced me to give you a trial, and you've shown a shepherd's parrion indeed. Snow and Storm told me, beyond what I saw, watching from afar. So, I offer another bargain, Tab. Will you be my apprentice and learn shepherding from the Master Shepherd?"

"I… the wolves killed some. I failed."

"Only three," Dort said. "And a fourth I had to heal. That's a full wolf pack you faced, young Tab, and surely you know by now, sheep are born hunting ways to die. You did well. Do you *want* to be a shepherd?"

Did he? All his earlier struggles and failures, the ridicule of other shepherds… and yet, those recent moments in which he saved a lamb from drowning, a ewe who was caught helpless upside down in a ditch, treated another's painful teat, had given him more satisfaction than anything.

"Yes," he said. "But I have a wife, and children, and I must care for them as well."

"I understand," Dort said. "Torre?"

"Almost here," Torre said. "And your own sheep as well."

Tab felt his shoulders sag.

His own sheep, scrawny, with patchy fleeces and sore feet… "They shouldn't mingle with yours," he said.

Dort's brows went up. "You said before they were sickly; we'll make them healthy. Tell me, is your name from your father?"

"No, his name was Nadel. It's a bricklayer term: straight-level. A good name." His own hung around his neck like a stone, weighing him down.

"And yours?" Torre asked, after a glance at Dort.

"Brickyard for… for a piece of broken brick. Useless."

"My apprentice cannot be named Useless," Dort said. "You are not useless now, and you will be a fine shepherd. You need a name in the shepherd's lineage. Will you accept one?"

61

Accept a new name? From the Master Shepherd? His head came up. Past Dort he saw three people coming down the path from the bowl's rim, accompanied by a few sheep half the size of Dort's and... not as sickly as he'd expected.

His wife was grinning; his children ran toward him. The sheep stopped, shuffled their hooves, staring ears-out at the large flock below.

"I'll call you Dorthakin," Dort said. "Come on—those sheep need our help."

Dorthakin. A name that held honor. The new apprentice with the new name followed his Master Shepherd up the path until, with one son clinging to each leg, they reached his wife and his tiny flock.

The sheep pushed forward. "More proof your parrion is shepherding," Dort said. "They know you and not me."

When Dort announced that his apprentice had met all his standards, Dorthakin and his wife and children—four now—and his flock of handsome, healthy sheep left the mountains and found unclaimed land where Dort had suggested. He and his family became famous in that region for the quality of their sheep and fleeces, and Dorthakin himself known for his expert knowledge. He taught every lad who wanted to learn, and his children followed in his path.

Author's Note on "Judgment"

I had not included a dragon in Paksworld before, but the invitation to write about a dragon in that universe was irresistible. Surely, just one dragon couldn't hurt. But once you invite one dragon into your imaginary world, more arrive. Was it the writer's wisdom, or folly, to let Dragon in? In this story, a naïve young man, his future father-in-law, and a search team of worried dwarves are all concerned about something that's gone missing. Dragon has a question: "Are you wise?"

Publication History: "Judgement" was originally published in *The Dragon Quintet*, Tor Books, 2003, ed. Marvin Kaye, and later reprinted in *Moon Flights*.

Judgment

"That's odd," Ker said, picking up the egg-shaped rock. "I never saw a rock shaped like an egg before." It was heavy, like any rock, cool in his hand. Smoother than any rock he'd ever seen.

"You find rocks like that in the hills west of here, lad," Tam said. He sounded as if he'd seen many such rocks before. "Someone dropped it," he said, looking around as if he expected to see that someone. "Gnome. Dwarf. Rockfolk would have something like that. And what'd they be doing here, I wonder? Never saw them this near the village; they need rocky hills to live in."

"They wouldn't drop it, not they." Ker turned the rock, rubbing it with his thumb. Stories said the rockfolk had grasping hands that never let go what they held. "It's smoother than most rocks anyway. Like someone'd polished it."

"Carried in a pocket with a hole in it. A sack—"

"I reckon as it belongs to someone, then," Ker said, putting the rock back on the path. "Best leave it be."

"For someone to stub a toe on in the dark?" Tam picked it up, hefted it, ran a calloused thumb over the smooth surface. "You're right, lad, it is smooth." He put it down just off the path, near a brambleberry tangle. "Now no one'll kick it in the dark and call a curse on us for leaving a tripstone, but it's easy enough to find, if whoever dropped it recalls what way they came."

Ker nodded and walked on, down past the brambleberry tangle, taking the steps made by its roots and those of the yellowwood thicket, steps worn into hollows by the feet of those who went daily from the creek up to the cow meadows and back. Under his bare feet, the warm earth turned cool, and then chill and damp as he neared the stream.

Tam followed; Ker could hear Tam's slower, more careful footfalls, the slight grunt as he came down the slope. Caution was in Tam's movements, in his words, as was proper for an older man, an Elder in the vill. Ker would not have worried about someone tripping on a rock in the path at night, though now Tam mentioned it, he knew he should worry. Others than humans used that path; the first humans here had found it bitten deep into the land, so that now the bushes and thickets towered over it, and near the creek he walked between walls of fern and flowers. The people of light used it, and the people of shadow, singers and unsingers, and the people of earth, those of the law and those of the forge. A curse from any of these might bring desolation to humans within its reach, and the curses of the Elders reached a long way.

Just beyond the old way marker, put there by no human hands in ancient times, he saw another of the odd egg-shaped rocks in the path. He made the sign to avert a curse. The rock remained. He stopped.

"Go on," said Tam from behind him, touching his shoulder.

"It's another one," Ker said.

"Another one what? Oh." Tam edged past Ker. "It's not the same color."

Ker had not noticed that; he had seen the shape only. Now he could not remember just what color the other one was. Stone colored, or he'd have noticed, but what color was stone? His mind threw up images of grey stone and brown, black stone and reddish yellow. This one was pale grey, speckled with dark.

"What if it is eggs?" he asked. "What if something lays stone eggs?"

Tam laughed, a harsh barking laugh. "What—you think maybe dwarfwives lay eggs?"

"I didn't say that." Ker stepped carefully around the rock. He wasn't going to pick it up this time. He'd averted a curse, or tried to, but handling things that might be cursed was a good way to catch bad luck anyway. He wished he hadn't touched the first one. "I only said—we found two. If they are eggs, what laid them?"

"They're not eggs. They're rocks." Tam bent down, picked up the rock, and shifted it from hand to hand. "This one's a little greyer. Heavier, not by much. Could be it has pretties inside. Some of them egg-shaped rocks over to Blackbone Hill has pretties inside. Gems, or near as need be."

Ker shivered. Blackbone Hill had a bad reputation, for all that some claimed to bring burning stone and valuable gemstones out of it. Stories were told about what lay under Blackbone Hill, what bones those were. A dragon, some said, had been killed there for his gold, and others said the dragon had died of old age, and still others argued that the dragon had choked on magegold. Tam had always said the stories were fool's gold, that only rock lay under the grass.

"Was there as a youngling," Tam went on. Ker knew that; everyone in the vill had heard Tam's stories of his travels. "A long ways off, and not much worth the trouble, but for the pretties." He hefted the rock in his hand. "I've half a mind to crack this open and see if it's that kind. Had to trade all the pretties I found at Blackbone for food, by the time I'd come home."

Ker shook his head. "What if it is something's egg? Bad luck, then, for sure."

"It's not an egg. Nothing lays stone eggs."

Nothing Tam knew of. Ker knew that he himself knew less than Tam, but surely even Tam did not know everything.

"We should ask somebody," he said, seeing Tam about to crack the rock egg against the old way marker that stood at the foot of the cut. The way marker came from the Elder People; it might be bad luck to break anything on it.

"Ask who?" Tam said.

That was the stopper. Tam knew more than anyone else Ker could think of; he was an Elder, but…

"Somebody," he said. "The singers, maybe?"

"Finders, keepers," Tam said, and his arm came down. The egg-shaped rock hit just on the edge of the way marker, and it broke open to show a serried rank of purple and white crystals.

"Pretties," Tam said with satisfaction. "Just as I thought. Here, Ker—you can have one." He probed with thick fingers and broke off a single crystal spike, about the length of his finger from knuckle to nail. He held it out.

Ker felt cold sweat break out on his face and neck. He could not refuse a gift from his future father-in-law, not without risking a quarrel, but he didn't want to touch that thing, whatever it was. He whipped off his neck cloth, and took the crystal in that. "I don't want to risk breaking it," he said. It was partly true, but the partial lie made a bad taste in his mouth. For courtesy, he looked closely at the crystal. Cloudy purple, the eight facets glinting in the light, the point narrowing abruptly at the tip…it looked sharp, and he did not test it with his finger. Carefully he folded the cloth around it and tucked it into his shirt, snugging his belt so it wouldn't fall out.

Tam took off his own neck cloth. "Good idea," he said. "Best not break the pretties. They're worth more unbroken." He wrapped the fragments of the rock, and put them in his shirt. Then he started off, leading the way this time. Ker did not see the next egg-shaped rock until Tam bent over, halfway across the gravelly ford of the creek, and picked it up. He showed it to Ker—this one was greenish-grey, streaked with darker green—before tucking it into his shirt with a grin. "If this'n has pretties too, I'm set for a long time. It's easy to trade pretties for 'most anything at the Greywood Fair. I'll pick up the other one tomorrow or the next day."

No more worries about who might've dropped it, Ker noticed. He followed Tam into the village, turning aside to his mother's house as Tam went straight on to his own. He lifted the hearthstone that guarded their treasures, and laid the pretty beside the armlet of bronze, the bronze pendant with a flower design, the string of glass beads he would give Tam's daughter the day they were wed, and eight silver bits that would, at his mother's death, be his inheritance and pay his cottage fee.

Then he went to sit in the village square, holding the staff of his approaching marriage, and endured until nightfall the taunts and teasing of those who tested a bridegroom's will and temper. It was hard not to respond when Dran's daughter kissed him full on the lips, or Roder's son told everyone about the time he had eaten a woods pear so fast he'd bitten a grub in two without noticing it, then thrown up. But this was the way of it. Lin had spent her time sitting in the square and now it was his turn; as he had sat on the judicar's bench and watched her, so now she sat on the same bench and watched him for any sign of impatience, bad temper, or unfaithfulness.

When full dark had come, and no one more bothered him, he went home and slept as usual until—in the darkest hours of night—he woke with a start, staring about him, bathed in cold sweat. Fragments of a dream swirled through his mind and vanished. Lin's face. Flame. Darkness. A great roaring that was almost music.

His ears hummed with the noise, as if someone had smacked him in the head with a rock. He tried to lie quietly, breathe slowly, return to sleep, but the humming itched at his ears and quieted only slowly. At last he slept.

In the morning he remembered waking, but nothing of the dream except that it was unpleasant. Today he would again spend the hours until homefaring with Tam, and then sit in the village square in the evening. He rose, fanned the embers of the fire into flame, then fetched water to boil. Lin's mother Ila, a guest in this house this five days, opened an eye and watched him, as his mother had guested with Tam for the days of Lin's testing and watched Lin. Ker measured grain into the pot, adding a pinch of salt from the salt-crock, then he left while the others rose. Tam was just coming out of his house.

"Guardians bless your rising," Ker said.

Tam grunted. "Guardians should bless my sleep instead. The water boils?"

"It boils," Ker said.

"Good. I'm hungry." Tam walked to Ker's mother's house, twitching his shoulders as if they hurt. Ker stood beside the door of Tam's house and waited, stomach growling, until Lin's little sister brought him a bowl of gruel and a small round of bread, lumpy and hard, the girl's own baking. Lin's would be better than this, he knew.

He ate it standing by the door, and the girl came to take away his bowl. He walked over to his mother's house, and waited until Tam came out, belching, his face red from the heat of the fire.

"Well, now, to work," Tam said. Today they would join the other men ditching a field near the creek, draining it. All morning, Ker hacked at the soggy soil with a blackwood spade, careful not to strain it to the breaking point. Old Ganner, who'd died before Midwinter, had carved the blackwood spade years back, and traded it to Ker's father for a tanned sheepskin. Ker knew himself lucky to have it.

Tam and the other men watched him as much as they worked themselves. No one liked ditching; it was hot, hard, heavy work that drew the back into tight knots, but the blackwood spade cut through the roots better than one of oak or ash.

Shortly after the noon break, Tam beckoned to Ker. Ker scraped the muck off the spade with the side of his foot and went to Tam's side. "Stay here, lad, and keep working. I'm going to check the cow pastures for us both," Tam said.

Ker's head throbbed. He knew what Tam would do. He would try to find that other egg-shaped stone, and break it open for more pretties. His heart sank, stonelike, and he found no words.

"You have the shoulders for digging," Tam said. "It's young man's work." He grinned and clapped Ker on the shoulder, then turned away.

Ker stabbed the ditch with the spade, more in worry than anger, and the spade groaned. Sorry, he thought to the wood, and stroked the handle. He looked closely at the shaft, but the grain had not split. Blackwood, best wood, supple and strong... blackwood made good bows as well as digging tools.

Tam came back in late afternoon, his hands empty and his face drawn into a knot like Ker's shoulders.

"You didn't sleep much last night," he said to Ker.

How had he known? "I had a bad dream," Ker said.

"You followed a dream out through the dark?" Tam asked.

Ker shook his head, confused. "I didn't go out," he said.

"It was gone," Tam said, not naming it. Ker knew what he meant.

"I did not take it," Ker said.

Tam shrugged. "Someone did. Rocks don't walk by themselves."

"Maybe the one who dropped it," Ker said.

"Maybe. No matter. I have the other for pretties." His sideways glance at Ker accused, though he said nothing more.

They went back to the village then, and Ker spent another evening in the square, with Lin on the bench watching him, and the young people standing around making jokes. Old Keth, Bari's mother, came and reminded everyone of the time he had spoiled a pot she was making, bumping her at her work. Lin's little sister reported that he had slurped his gruel that very morning, gobbling like a wild pig of the forest. He bore it patiently, as Lin had borne it when his mother told that Lin had made a tangle in the weaving.

That night he dreamed again: fire, smoke, Lin's face, noise. Again he woke struggling against that fear, and again his ears hummed for a time before he could sleep again. In the morning he knew he had had the same dream again, but still remembered nothing of it. That frightened him: to repeat a dream meant something, but he could not interpret a dream he could not remember.

That day he finished the ditch before it was time to sit in the square, and decided to cool off in the creek. Tam was talking to the older men, in the shade of the trees. Ker waved, mimed splashing, and walked off to the creek. Upstream from the ford, the creek had scooped out a bowl waist deep at this time of year.

Under the trees the sun no longer bit his shoulders, but the air lay still and hot. His feet followed the path as his mind cast itself ahead into the cool water. The scent of damp and fresh growth filled his nose, promising comfort. He came to the ford, where the water scarcely wet the top of his foot, and turned aside to the pool, stripping off his shirt and trews to hang them on the bushes to one side.

He eased into the water, murmuring the thanks appropriate to the merin of the creek, and splashed it over his head and shoulders. Something tickled his heart foot, then the other. Slowly he sank down in the water, crouching, until only his head was out. He had always loved the way the water's skin looked, seen from just above it like this. Its surface would have looked flat from above, but now, in the wavering reflection of the trees overhead, he could see its true shape, the grain of its flow. On his back, the current's gentle push, and between his legs the water flowing away downstream, past the village lands, beyond into lands unknown.

He let his eyes close and listened. No sound of breeze in the trees, no leaf rustle. Something moved on a tree trunk; he heard the scritch of claws on bark.

He had known Tam all his life. Cautious Tam, careful Tam, thoughtful Tam, perhaps not as wise as Granna Sofi, but then she was older, deeper in wisdom. Now he wondered if he knew Tam at all. And if he knew too little of Tam, what of his daughter Lin? If Tam could turn grasping, so late in life, would Lin draw back her hand from life-giving? Would she be a fist and not an open hand after all?

He wished his father had lived. He could not talk to his

mother about this, not now. She had asked the ritual questions, back before Lin sat in the square, and he had said yes, he was sure the Lady's blessing lay on Lin and on their union. He had been sure.

He was not sure now. He knew only that he woke each night in the darkest hours, after foul dreams, with strange music humming in his head.

He squeezed his eyes shut and sank below the surface. Cool water lifted the strands of his hair, washing away the sweat and grime. Cool water supported him everywhere. If he were a fish, he could live in this cool cleanliness always, in this silence. He opened his eyes underwater and watched tiny silver bubbles from his nose rise past his eyes. Air seeking air, its own kind. He was not waterkind or airkind, neither fish nor bird.

His lungs ached. He lifted slightly, rolling his head back to catch a breath, and blinked the water out of his eyes. Even as he heard a startled hiss, he saw them.

Two squat shapes, half the height of men but not boys, stood in the shallows staring at him. One muttered at the other, no tongue he knew. Of course not: they were Elders, rockfolk Elders. He knew that from the tales, every detail of which came back to him in that instant. Squat, broad, long-haired, bearded, teeth like stone pegs, hands and feet overlarge for their height. Clothed in leather and metal. Armed with metal weapons. And angry. In the tales, the rockfolk were always angry, usually with a human who invaded their fastnesses or stole something from them.

He was aware of a chill from more than the water, and aware too of his own nakedness. His clothes... one of the rockfolk had them now, stretching and poking at his shirt with a finger he knew would tear it... yes. He heard it rip. That one sniffed at the shirt, and wrinkled a broad nose; it gave a harsh sound that might've been a laugh. The other answered in its language.

Then came the sound of someone else brushing through the bushes, crackling leaves underfoot, nearer and nearer. The two rockfolk looked at each other and vanished. His shirt fell to the water's surface, where the current took and folded it, then slid it downstream, slowly, rumpling over the shallows. Ker lurched forward out of the pool, back to the shallows, and made a grab for it. The wet mass resisted, and he yanked it up just as Tam broke through the bushes and stood on the bank scowling at him.

"Looking for another?" Tam asked.

"No, I was hot," Ker said. "I was in the pool..."

"You're not in the pool now. What have you got in that shirt?" Tam sounded almost as angry as the rockfolk had looked.

"Nothing," Ker said. He held it up, wrung out the water, and spread it. The rent was a hand long, a three-cornered tear.

"Something made that—" Tam came into the ford, looking around as if he expected to find another of the odd rocks, as if one might have fallen through that hole in Ker's shirt.

"It was the dwarf," Ker said. "Two rockfolk were on the ford when I came up from the water. One of them had my shirt. Then I heard someone coming, and they were gone. My shirt fell into the water—"

Tam's eyebrows rose. "Gone? Where?" he asked. "I don't see any rockfolk." He looked around, then back at Ker.

"I don't know," Ker said. "They just... weren't there. Maybe it was magic."

"Maybe there weren't any rockfolk," Tam said, his voice hard. "Maybe that's why I didn't see them.

"I saw them," Ker said. "I came up from the water and they were there, in the ford, with my shirt—one of them poked a hole in it—"

"And you didn't say anything?"

"No. I couldn't think—"

"Mmm." Tam didn't say more, but Ker suspected he hadn't believed a word of it. He didn't know what to say, how to convince Tam that he had seen dwarves, and they had disappeared. "I think I need a soak too, lad," Tam said. "Best you get back to the village, now, and sit your time."

Ker nodded and fetched the rest of his clothes from the bush he'd laid them on. He put on the trews and draped his wet shirt on his head. He would have to put it on to enter the village, but it might be drier by the time he'd made it to the clearing. And he'd have to explain that rent to his mother. Would she believe him about the dwarves or would she be like Tam? Perhaps he could tell her simply that the shirt had gotten torn, and nothing more.

His mother turned the shirt in her hands, examining the ripped cloth, seeming to half-listen to his explanation. "I will fix it this evening," she said. "Don't worry about it." Ker felt guilty. Though he was almost sure that not telling everything true was not the same as telling something untrue, that *almost* pricked him like a thorn.

He thought so hard about that, sitting in the square that evening, that he scarcely noticed what anyone said or did. The Elders said that lies ripped the fabric of the community, destroyed the trust between people on which community rested. Between him and his mother stood the not-telling about the rockfolk. Between him and Lin's family stood the lies Tam had told and Tam's grasping at what was not his. Like father like daughter, like mother like son. Did he want to be married forever to the daughter of someone like Tam... the daughter of Tam himself?

He stumbled home in the dark, finally, more miserable than he had been since his father died, and lay down sure he would not sleep. At least he would not dream, if he did not sleep.

Despite himself, he dozed off after a time, and woke to voices whispering in the dark, just out of clear hearing. His heart pounded; he lay still, trying to breathe quietly so that he could hear what they said. Dry voices, evoking the rustle of winter leaves crisped by frost and blown by wind, or the little streaked birds of open grassland in midsummer. The blurred edges of speech sharpened slowly; he could hear more and more... but he could not understand. He shook his head, blinked against the dark, but the voices still spoke words he did not know. Then he heard his own name, clear within the bird-sounds of the voices. Once, and then again, "Ker." And "Lin" and "Tam" as well.

Blood rushed in his ears; he lost the voices in its rhythmic noise. He shivered, suddenly drenched in sweat and cold. Voices that knew his name when he did not know their speech. That must be the Elders, but which race? The people of light were the Singer's children; they had singing voices. The people of darkness, once also of the Singer's tribe, had fallen away but retained their beauty, it was said. The rockfolk spoke loud and deep; the people of the law with almost mincing precision. None of these fit the sound he heard.

He sat up and peered through the dark at the hearthstone. It must be the pretty Tam had given him; that must be what caused this. He must get rid of it. He thought of throwing it in the creek, burying it in the woods.

"Fool!" came the voice, now in his own tongue. "Put it back."

Back? He tried to remember just where on the path Tam had picked it up—just this side of the waystone, yes—and the voice crackled like a fire as it said, "No! Fool! Restore, restore..."

Restore what? How?

Above the hearthstone now, a blue flame danced where no

fire had been laid. Behind it, the banked embers of last night's fire sighed and collapsed with a soft puff of ash; the air chilled again, and the blue flame brightened. Ker could not take his eyes from it. Within it, a tiny shape he could not quite see clearly twisted and turned.

"Put it back together. Every piece. Make whole, make well. Else—" A blast of fear shook him, shattering his concentration, implying every disaster that could come to him and his family, his whole village.

Then it vanished, leaving only a blurry afterimage against the dark, and Ker lay back on his pallet, sweating and shivering, until the first dawnlight crept through the windows. He put the water on and started the porridge as usual. He would have to talk to Tam about this, and he had no idea how to say what he must say.

Tam came out looking even grumpier than the day before. "Guardians bless your rising," Ker said.

"Guardians should bless my sleep," Tam said, as he had before. That was not the ritual greeting. Was he also having bad dreams?

"Honored one," Ker began, then stopped as Tam rounded on him.

"Don't you start!" he said. "You're not my son-in-law yet." He strode off to Ker's mother's house before Ker could say anything more.

When Lin's little sister came out with his bowl of lumpy gruel and piece of bread, she shook her head at him. "Da's angry with you," she said. "What did you do wrong?"

"I don't know," Ker said. Did Tam still think he had taken that other rock from the brambleberry patch? The only wrong he knew of was keeping the pretty, but Tam had given it to him.

"Yes, you do," Lin's sister said, staring at him wide-eyed. "You have a liar's look. I'll tell Linnie."

That was all he needed now, for Lin to believe him untrue. If she didn't already, if her father had not convinced her.

"I do not know why your father is angry with me," he said. "That is the truth."

She shifted from foot to foot, staring at him. "It sounds true, but something is wrong. Da isn't sleeping well—we're all tossing and turning and when I asked him what was wrong, he said it was you. You are a thief, he said."

"A thief! Me?" That accusation bit like an ax blade. "I am no thief. I have taken nothing—" He almost said: It was your father, but stopped himself in time.

"That sounds true," she said. Now her face changed, crumpling into misery. "But Da—my Da—he tells the truth."

Sometimes, Ker thought. Not always. He would not tell the child, though; a child's trust in a parent was too precious to risk.

"You must have done something wrong," the child persisted. "Or he wouldn't be angry with you."

"I will ask him," Ker said. "I will find out and make it right."

"Truly?"

"Truly. You will see."

"Lin is crying," the child said, then ducked back inside.

Ker took a long breath of morning air flavored with cooking smells, and struggled to finish his gruel and bread. It would be discourteous, an insult to Lin's entire family, if he did not finish the food. It lay in his belly like a stone. When he was done, he walked back to his own house and waited for Tam to emerge.

"We have to talk," Tam said, when he came out. His eyes looked red as well as his face. His hard hand on Ker's arm felt hot as a cooking pot.

"Yes," Ker said. "We do." He didn't resist as Tam pushed him away from the house, toward the woods and then into them. Before Tam could say anything, Ker spoke. "It's wrong."

"What?"

"That… thing. That rock. With the pretties. It's wrong. You have to put it back together, fix it, put it back."

Tam snorted. "So you can just happen to find it and take it for yourself? Not likely, my lad. That's just the sort of sneaky lie I'd expect from someone like you."

"I had a dream," Ker said, ignoring the insult. "Three nights in a row, and last night I woke and heard voices, and saw a flame on the hearthstone…"

"You didn't bank the fire right, and it burned through. You're lazy as well as a liar, Ker. I've done my best by you, but you needed a father years ago to teach you right from wrong…"

The unfairness of this stopped Ker's tongue in his mouth. Tam went on. "It has to stop, Ker. I didn't say anything because I thought, it's not his fault, he's just a boy, he'll learn. But after that day on the trail… you sneaking back to find more…"

"I wasn't," Ker said. He could hear the tension in his own voice.

"Lying to me about your shirt… did you think I couldn't tell you were lying? Rockfolk tore it, you said, when there were no rockfolk to be seen. You had something in that shirt, something heavy, and when you heard me coming you threw it into deep water. I say it was the other rock. You found something, saw something…" Tam's voice carried complete conviction; he had convinced himself that it was all Ker's fault.

"I was hot," Ker said. He thought, but didn't say, that he'd been working a lot harder than Tam, out in the sun. "I went to cool off in the creek. I saw the rockfolk and then they were gone. That's all." Even to himself that sounded sullen and secretive; he saw again in his mind the rockfolk in their leather, their great axes, their sudden disappearance.

"Last year I might've believed that, Ker. This year… this year I think you want my daughter and my pretties as well. Maybe my life."

"Your—Tam, what are you talking about?"

"Sitting outside my house putting a curse on my sleep, and then claiming you have bad dreams—"

"I didn't—"

"Whispering mean things, putting ugly pictures in my head. That's not what I want in a son-in-law, a witchy man, an ill-wisher, a doomsayer. I'm taking back my daughter's troth, and I want that pretty I gave you before I knew about you."

"But I didn't do what you think," Ker said. "It's the pretties—they send the bad dreams, I'm sure of it. That's why we need to put it back together, so it will stop doing that, so the village will be safe. That's what it told me."

"Pretty rocks don't give bad dreams," Tam said. "They don't talk in the night, or make a man see his children flayed and burning… bad things. Ill-wishers do that. You can't fool me, Ker, trying to blame all that on a rock. My Ila woke in the night and saw you sitting up by the window—easy enough for you to slide in and out, with your pallet right there." He made a chopping motion with his hand. "No daughter of mine will marry a man who sends evil dreams. Now—for the last time—give me that pretty I gave you, and understand the troth is broken. You have today to make your peace with your mother, for this evening I will tell the Elders why the troth is broken. It would be best for you if you were gone by then."

"Gone—?" Ker stared.

"Wake up, boy. Whatever dream of power you had is over.

We will not tolerate an ill-wisher in this vill, not while I'm an Elder. If I were not a kind man, forbearing, I would kill you where you stand."

"But I didn't—"

"Enough. Come now, and return to me that which is mine." Tam's hot, hard hand closed again on Ker's arm, and dragged him back toward the village and his house. Ker stumbled along, his mind in a whirl of confusion.

The other men had gone out to the fields already, but two children and their mother stared as Tam strode along. Ker kept up now, but Tam still held his arm as if he might try to escape. At Ker's mother's house, he heard his mother inside chanting the baking rhyme.

"I can't go in now," Ker muttered. Men did not intrude when women were singing the dough up from the trough. Tam must know that. Tam merely grunted, glaring into the distance, and kept his hold on Ker's arm. Ker sneaked a glance at him. Tam's face, his ears, his neck, were all as red as if he'd worked all day in the hot sun. Was he fevered, was that the source of his wrong thinking?

When Ker's mother finished the chant, Tam cleared his throat loudly and called to her. "We men must enter."

"Come, then," she said. Tam gave Ker a shove, pushing him through the doorway first.

"What is it?" she asked. She covered the dough with a cloth, and wiped her hands.

"Get the pretty," Tam said to Ker, then turned to his mother. "I have broken the troth, Rahel," he said. "My daughter shall not marry your son."

"Why—what is it? What's wrong? Ker—?"

"It gives me pain to say this," Tam said, putting his fist over his heart. "Your son is an ill-wisher."

"No!" His mother gave him one frantic look, then turned back to Tam, her hands twisting in her skirt. "No, you're wrong. Not Ker. He's always been a sweet boy—"

"He lies," Tam said loudly. "He lied to me. He tried to steal. And he sneaks out at night to lay a curse on my sleep and give me bad dreams."

"I don't believe it," she said. "Not Ker."

"Three nights I've had of broken sleep, and voices whispering, and in the morning he is there to wish me well, with a look on his face that would curdle milk."

"Ker…?" Again she looked at Ker, her face pale in the dimness.

"Get the pretty, damn you!" Tam roared. He seemed to fill the room.

Ker scrabbled at the stone and pried it up. The pretty looked smaller, dusty, in the room's dimmer light. He picked it up in bare fingers, and nearly dropped it again—it was so heavy and so very cold. He held it to the light for a moment; in the cloudy center he could almost see something, some tiny writhing shape. Did it really move, or did he imagine it?

"Give it to me," Tam said. Before Ker could comply, Tam grabbed his hand and forced the fingers open. Tam's breath whooshed in, and back out on "Ahhhhh…." He took it and put it in his pocket.

"What is that?" asked his mother. "That thing—a rock?"

"Some rocks have pretties inside," Tam said. "They bring a good price at the fair, pretties do. I found such a rock when your son was with me. I broke it open, and gave him one of the pretties inside, because he was to be my son-in-law, and in token of the care I had for him. That was before I knew about him."

"I can't believe what you say," his mother said.

"It doesn't matter what you believe," Tam said. "I will tell the Elders tonight why the troth is broken. I told him, make peace with your family and then leave before that meeting. For I will not have an ill-wisher in this vill."

"But—surely Ker may tell his story…"

"If he is that foolish, he may. But who would believe a liar and a thief, someone who has put a curse on the sleep of my household? The Elders respect me."

"Ker, did you lie to Tam? About anything? At any time?" The look in her eyes expected *no* but though he had lied to Tam he could not lie to his mother.

"When he gave me the pretty, I did not want to touch it," Ker said. "I was afraid of bad luck. So that is one reason I wrapped it in my neck cloth, and I did not tell him that reason."

"That's not what I mean and you know it," Tam said. "I found you in the creek ford, hunting for more—"

"I was not," Ker said.

"Spinning that yarn about rockfolk," Tam said. "As if I couldn't see with my own eyes that you were alone, scrabbling in the rocks of the ford. No rockfolk upcreek or down, uptrail or down. Did they fly up into the air like birds?"

Ker's mother looked at him as if he should have the answer. "I don't know," he said to her; he knew Tam would not believe him. "They just—weren't there, after I heard Tam coming."

"Not a skillful liar," Tam said. "If you think to make your way as a storyteller, Ker, you must do better than that. But never mind—a self-confessed liar, a thief, an ill-wisher—I am going now, and you may tell your mother whatever ice-stories you wish before nightfall. They will melt by day, as all such do." He strode out of the house, and the heat of the day went with him.

"Ker, I don't understand," his mother said. In her face he saw lines he had never noticed before. "You know that lies are wrong…"

He could not bear it, that she would think he was what Tam had said. "Please," he said. "I did not lie. Let me tell you about it."

She did not quite shrug, leaning on her work table. Ker told her all about that day—only a few days ago, it was. Finding the first stone, and the second and third, Tam's actions and his own feeling of dread, his unwillingness to touch the pretty. His nightmares, his awareness of Tam's unfounded suspicions, and finally—last night—his realization that someone—something—demanded that the broken rock be fitted together again, mended, and then restored to its former location. Tam's anger this morning, and his accusations; his refusal to believe the rock and its pretties were dangerous.

"It is like a tale out of legend," she said when he had fallen silent. "Strange rocks and frightening dreams and dwarves that say nothing but disappear when someone else comes. Tam is respected, as he said, a father and Elder, a man with knowledge beyond our fields. You are scarce old enough to wed, and you have admitted lying to him about your reason for not touching the pretty."

"It wasn't a lie," Ker said. "I just didn't tell him all. And I didn't steal anything, or curse his sleep. The rock did that."

"It was a kind of lie," his mother said. "Not telling the whole truth, and now see what comes of it. He can say truly that you were not always true. As for the rest, I believe you." She sighed, wiped her hands on her apron, and shook her head. "But will anyone else?"

His heart sank. "Surely they will. They have known me from

my birth. They know I tell the truth. They know you. And even if they do not believe me—must I really go? Leave the village?"

"I think you must, Ker. Tam will not give you—nor any of us—peace until you're gone." She seemed calmly sure of this.

"They know me," Ker said again. It seemed impossible that this might make no difference. "Why do you think they will think I'm lying?"

"They know Tam better, or think they do." His mother picked up a hand-broom and swept the hearth where the ashes had spilled out onto it.

"I have to talk to them myself. It isn't fair..."

"Fairness is for the gods, Ker. We are not gods, to know for certain what is and is not fair."

"But if Tam doesn't put the rock back together, something bad will happen. Not just to him, to Lin and maybe the whole village. They should be warned." He was sure of it now, sure that his dream was right, that Tam was wrong about more than his own conduct.

His mother sighed. "It's you should be warned, Ker. You have never seen a shunning; you don't know... if you talk to them, and they side with Tam, we will both be shunned away."

"And if I don't, and the village burns or the rockfolk come in anger? Will that not be my fault if I have not warned them?"

She sighed again, shaking her head. "It is the cleft stick, and we are fairly in the trap. For you are my son; what they judge you to be, they will judge I have made you. I tell you, Ker, it is never easy for a vill to choose a young man's story over that of a wise Elder. And it is a hard thing to be thrust out into the world alone at my age."

As he watched, she began to set in piles all their belongings, and Ker realized she meant to leave... for the smaller pile would fit in the pack basket his father had used to carry fleeces to market or in the basket she herself used to carry sticks or berries or nuts home from the wood.

Slowly at first, he moved to help her, thinking ahead to what they would need if they were cast out. Food, clothes, cooking things, tools. Everything he touched brought memories of the one who had made it, and stabbed his heart with the possibility of loss. It must not happen. He must find the words to say, words to convince the others that he was right about the danger. He tried not to let himself think about Lin, about never seeing her again.

When the men came in from work that evening, Ker stood outside his house with his mother. Tam glared at him, even redder of face than in the morning. "I told you—" he began, but Ker interrupted.

"I ask the village Elders to meet," Ker said, as loudly as Tam. "Tam has a grievance against me, and I have my own words to say, a warning to give."

The other men looked at each other. For the first time Ker wondered if Tam had said anything to them during the day's work. How had he explained Ker's absence?

"After you sit your time?" Beryan asked, glancing at Tam. He was senior of the men in that group.

"No," Ker and Tam said together.

"I am not sitting my time," Ker said. "I abide the meeting."

"Not for long," Tam said, and strode away to his own house. The other men looked at Ker. He felt the force of their stares, but said nothing.

"At starshine, then," Beryan said. "Lady's grace on you, until." He turned away and the others followed.

Ker's mother set out a supper that Ker saw included most

of the perishables in the larder. He tried to eat, but the food sat uneasily in his stomach. Outside, the day waned, and he knew word of something unusual would have spread. He and his mother came out into the dusk and looked up, waiting until the first star appeared.

The oldest men and women in the village had gathered around the well, holding candles; others, he knew from murmurs and shufflings in the dark, hung back in the houses or between them. No one spoke to him. As Ker and his mother walked toward them, the Elders drew back into two wings on either side of the well.

"Guardians bless the hour," Granna Keth said. Her voice quavered.

"Guardians bless the air that gives breath," Granna Sofi said.

"Guardians bless the earth that gives grain," Othrin said. He was eldest of the men.

"Guardians bless the water that gives life," Ker's mother said.

"Guardians bless the fire that gives light," Ker said.

"Lady's grace," they all said together.

Then Othrin said, "Tam says he has a grievance against you, Ker, and you have acknowledged such a grievance. As he is elder, he will speak first."

Tam began at once, in a voice thick with anger. His version of events now included a long-festering suspicion that Ker had asked permission to court Lin only because he sought to rob her father… that Ker had always intended to go back and steal the special rocks, that Ker had learned sorcery while wandering in the woods and used it to harm anyone he disliked. A fatherless boy, Tam said, despite the care he and every other man had given him… such boys might easily find a way to learn evil things.

Ker could feel, as if it were a chill wind, the suspicion of the others as Tam blamed him for one mishap after another. Yes, he had been in the field that spring when Malo stepped on a rake, but no one then had blamed him. Malo had left his own rake tines up and forgotten where he laid it. Yes, he had been at the well when two scuffling boys slipped and one cut his chin on the well-curbing, but their mother had scolded them, not Ker. Now she eyed Ker askance.

By the time his turn came to speak, he felt smothered under the weight of their dislike, their anger. Had they always disliked him? He was no longer sure.

He did his best to tell his own story, straight from first seeing the stones to the uneasy dreams, and his conviction that it was wrong to keep the stones, that they must be returned to their real owner.

"Wrong! Yes, wrong to have an ill-wisher—" Tam burst out.

Othrin put out a hand.

"Let the lad say his say," he said.

Ker said it again, trying to make them understand, but Tam's obvious anger and certainty drew their attention.

"Liar!" Tam said finally. "I was there. I saw no rockfolk at the ford. The first rock I found was gone, and only you knew where it was."

"They were there," Ker said. "Two of them, this high." His hands sketched their size. "They had my shirt; one of them sniffed at it and poked it and it tore. It is all true, what I told you then. I do not know how they disappeared—how would I know the ways of rockfolk?—but they did. You must believe me—you must put the rocks back, all the pieces together, or something bad will happen."

"Bad things will happen to a vill with a liar and an ill-wisher in it," Tam said. "A man who lies about one thing lies about all."

Ker saw heads nodding. "A rock is a rock—look—" He showed the unbroken rock to the elders, who leaned closer; several touched it. A drop of hot wax fell on the rock, and Ker flinched. Tam went on. "It is easy for him to say that bad dreams woke him, but I tell you that he did not sleep because he was putting bad dreams into my sleep. Ill-wishing. There is the bad thing."

A low mutter of agreement, heads moving from side to side. At the back of the group, several women turned their backs on his mother. His heart went cold.

"I did not..." he began, but Othrin held up his hand.

"It is not right that a young man not yet wed should tell the Elders what to do," he said. "You make threats as if you were a forest lord or city king, but you are a boy we knew from birth. Even if the rockfolk come here, I have no doubt Tam will restore to them their property, if indeed it is their property. They would have no complaint against us. As for the rock, it looks like a rock to me. It is shaped like an egg, but what of that? You all but accuse Tam of stealing and lying, when he is your elder and would have taken you into his family. It is not right." He looked around the circle of Elders, and they all nodded.

"Go out, Ker, and do not return. You are not of us any longer." He glanced again at the others, who nodded again. "And your mother as well. Like mother, like son; like son, like mother. Take her with you, liar and ill-wisher." He turned his back. The others turned their backs, until Ker faced a dark wall of backs. Only Tam still faced him, his red face almost glowing in the dark.

"Drive them out now!" Tam said. "They will ill-wish us all—"

"Not by night," Othrin said without turning around. "We are not people who would turn a widow and orphan out to face the perils of night, no matter what they did. But be gone by the time the sun's light strikes the well-cover, Ker. After that, it shall be as Tam wishes."

Ker and his mother walked back to their house in silence and darkness; the others had all gone inside and barred doors against them.

"Well," said his mother when they were inside, with their own door barred. She did not light a candle; Ker remembered that their few candles were in the packs already. "We must sleep, and rise early." Her voice was calm, empty of all emotion.

"Mother—" he began.

She put up her hand. "No. I do not want to talk. I want to remember my life here, before it ends forever."

That night Ker had no frightening dreams, but woke in the dark before dawn to hear his mother sobbing softly. "I'm sorry," he said into the darkness.

"It is not your fault," she said. "Not entirely. I could wish you had not lied even in so small a thing as leaving out one reason for an action. But if you are awake, let us go. I have heard the first birds in the woods, and I want to be long gone by daybreak."

They rose and felt their way to the bundles packed the day before, unbarred the door, and came out into the fresh smells of a summer night. Overhead, the stars still burned, but less bright than in deep night. Ker could see the dark bulks of the other houses, the looming darkness of the wood, and the pale thread of path leading toward the fields. The dust was dew-damp under his feet.

He could not believe he was seeing his home for the last time, but even as he hesitated, he heard a cry from Tam's house up the lane. Light blossomed behind the windows, around the door, and Tam's angry voice grew louder. Ker took a step back, onto the path.

"Come," his mother said. "Come now."

Still he hesitated. And then Tam flung open the door of his house—outlined against the light inside—and yelled into the night. "Damned ill-wisher—he's still here, he's putting his evil on the village even now—burn him out! Burn him out, I say!"

Up and down the lane Ker saw light appear in windows and doors as men and women snatched up brands from their fires and waved them into bright flame.

"Come on," his mother said, tugging at his arm. Ker turned and stumbled after her as fast as he could under the load he carried. Behind, he could hear angry voices. As they reached the turn into the first field, he glanced back and saw that the twinkling brands were together in a mass near their house.

"We must go to the hills," his mother said. They had crossed the ford, stumbling on rocks that seem to have grown all points in the darkness and now stood among the bushes that edged one of the grazing areas. "My mother's mother's people came that way; I will have kin-sibs somewhere in that direction."

"But it's the wrong way," Ker said. "That's the path the stones were on, that the rockfolk were on. We should stay far away from it and the curse they bore."

"If we see any stones, we won't touch them," his mother said. "And we have none, so the rockfolk—if they were seeking the stones—should not bother us."

He was not so sure, but they had to go somewhere: they could not just stand there arguing. The smoke from their burning house trailed after them like an evil spirit. He could hear the villagers yelling in the distance; they might pursue. His mother started off and Ker followed, bending under the load as they climbed away from the creek and back onto the trail.

By afternoon, they were beyond the vill's farthest cow pastures; taller hills loomed ahead. The well-trodden path had thinned to a track scarcely wide enough for one. When they came to a little dell with trees arching over a spring, Ker's mother left the trail and went down to it. She sat down in the shade with a sigh. Her face sagged with weariness. "We will sleep here," she said. "It has been too long since I walked the day away. Go and find us some firefuel, Ker, while I sing the water."

Ker shrugged out of the pack basket's straps and leaned it against a tree. He paused to take a drink from one of the waterskins they had filled the day before, then left everything with his mother and climbed back to the trail and looked around. Back down the trail, a narrow fringe of trees and shrubs they had passed a handspan of sun before. Far in the distance he could just see a smudge of smoke where the village lay. Ahead, the woods in the dell widened up the slope to meet the trail ahead. That was closer, and he'd be coming downhill with the load.

He walked up the trail, light-footed now without the load on his back, and turned aside where the scrub met the trail. He found a rocky watercourse, now dry, though the trees overhead indicated water somewhere underground. Tiny ferns decorated cracks in the grey rock. One delicate-petaled pink flower hugged the ground just below that ledge. All the rocks were rough, grey, blocky; none were egg-shaped. Lodged against one of the rocks was a tangle of sticks, all sizes, and all dry. He pulled a thong from his pocket and bound them together. Working his way down the dry creek-bed, he found here a branch that he could break over his knee, and there another flood-tangle.

As he neared the dell, he heard his mother moving about, but no more singing.

"I'm coming," he called, just in case.

"Come, then," she said.

He worked his way slowly toward her, the bulky bundle catching on vines and undergrowth. Just above the spring, a rock ledge jutted from the watercourse, flood-worn to smoothness. Here was another tangle of sticks—a quick flood, he thought, must have dropped it before the water could push it over the edge. It looked almost like a house of sticks. Perhaps some animal—? He bent over awkwardly and picked them up. Blackwood, yellowwood, blood oak, silver ash. Odd. He hadn't seen any blackwood or silver ash uphill. But they burned well; he carried them in one hand as he found a way down and around the ledge into the dell.

After a meager supper of bread wrapped on sticks and cooked over the fire, Ker sat watching the coals as the fire died down. No need to bank the fire; they would be moving on at dawn in the morning. His mother, tired out by the day's walk, had already fallen asleep, warded from the night's chill by their blanket. He was tired too, drained by all that had happened. His head dropped forward on his chest, and he dozed.

Pain shocked him awake, stinging blows to his face; he heard his mother cry out and struggled up from sleep to find himself facing a blazing fire and four rockfolk as angry as any in the tales. Two held his mother, and two more confronted him. His cheeks burned with the slaps that had wakened him.

"Where are they?" asked one. His voice could have been rocks grinding together.

Ker blinked sleep out of his eyes. "What?" he asked. Another slap.

"You stink of them," the dwarf said. "Do not lie. You have held what we seek: where are they?"

He realized what they meant. "I don't have them," he said.

"Who does, then? Where are they?"

He hesitated, and the other one slapped him again. Again his mother cried out. "Don't hurt her!" Ker said, suddenly as much angry as scared. "She's my mother—"

"She is not hurt," the first one said. "She is scared."

"Ker..." came his mother's voice.

"Don't hurt her," he said again, surprised to hear his own voice deep and firm. "It's not right."

"It was not right of you to steal what was not yours," the dwarf said.

"I didn't," Ker said. *It was Tam* hovered behind his lips, but he stopped himself. Tam had been unjust to him, but he would not help that ill seed grow.

"But you know what we seek. How do you know, if it was not you who took them?"

Ker glanced at his mother. The whites of her eyes glinted; he could not read her expression as the light of leaping flames came and went across it. Which was worse, to betray Tam to the rockfolk, or see his mother frightened... hurt... dead?

Another slap rocked his head, more bruise than sting. "Who?" the dwarf demanded.

"What will you do to that one?" Ker asked. His mouth hurt; he tasted the salt that meant his mouth was bleeding. "It is not for me to bring someone else into trouble."

"Ha!" The dwarf facing him straightened. Standing upright, he was taller than Ker sitting down, but not by much. Firelight glinted on the metal in his harness; he looked strong as a tree. "You invade our lands, steal our patterans for firewood, despoil our spring, and you worry about getting someone else in trouble? You have enough trouble of your own."

"But the trail is open to all…I thought," Ker said. "And what is a patteran?"

The dwarf grunted. "The trail, yes. So the treaties ran, from the days the first men came here: the trail is for all, folk of the air and folk of the forest and folk of the rocks. This is not the trail. The trail is there—" a thick finger pointed upslope. "This is not the trail. You took our patterans—our trail markers—for firewood—"

Ker remembered the curious shape of the "flood drift" he'd found on the rock ledge; his face must have shown that memory because the dwarf nodded sharply. "Yes. Leaving aside the other, that is a thief's action. And you have polluted this spring—"

"We did not," Ker said. "My mother sang the blessing."

The dwarf cocked his head. "Did she now? And does human woman not know that such a blessing sung by a woman must not be heard by a man, and sung by a man must not be heard by a woman?" He looked across at Ker's mother, now sitting slumped between the other two rockfolk. She said nothing.

"I left so she could sing it—to gather firewood," Ker said. "I did not hear it."

"And you took our patteran."

"I didn't know it was a marker—a patteran," Ker said.

"What matters that? You took it. If not for your fire, and your snores, which made you easy to find, we might have gone astray from the path our comrades left for us. But we found you, and you have knowledge we seek. So, human, let us come back to that: if indeed you did not take our treasure, why do you bear its smell? Who took it? Where can this person be found? For if we find it not, and quickly, great peril falls on all this land."

Ker believed that. Between his dreams and the rockfolk, he believed absolutely in the certainty of some dire fate.

"I will tell you," he said. "But you must not hurt my mother."

"That is our business, not yours. Yet I say that it is not our habit to harm human women. Or human men, if they do us no harm."

With a last glance at his mother, Ker told the story yet again. "I was coming back from the cow pasture with an older man, the father of my betrothed," Ker said. "I saw a strange rock in the path..." He told about the egg-shaped rocks, about Tam's reaction to the second and third rock. "He said it was like rocks from Blackbone Hill."

"Blackbone Hill! Your people travel so far?"

"Most do not, but he had, he said, when he was young. And he had found round rocks with pretty crystals inside, he said, and he wondered if this might be such a one. So he—he broke it on the waystone. It had pretty things inside; he gave me one."

The dwarf growled something Ker could not understand. Then: "Fool! Idiot! Stupid child of dirt and water! On the *way marker*! Tell me, is this person accounted a simpleton, one with scant mind?"

"No... he is an Elder."

The dwarf stared, bushy brows raised high. "This man is what you call wise?" Then he scowled. "I do not believe it! No one who has been to Blackbone Hill could fail to know the dangers of such things."

"He said they fetched a good price at the fair." Curiosity finally got past fear. "What are they, those rocks?"

"Rocks." The dwarf turned away and tipped out the pack basket. Pots clattered onto the ground. "Is it in here?"

"No! I gave it back to him," Ker said. "I told you—" The dwarf paid no attention, pawing through the pile... skeins of wool twisted on wooden knitting needles, his mother's spare skirt, two aprons, his spare shirt and trews, his winter shoes, last year's straw rosette from above the fireplace, the jar of bread starter, the jar of lard, the waterskins, the sack of beans. Those hard, stubby fingers probed through the pile, found the bracelet and tossed it aside, found the silver bits and paused.

"Where came these? Did you sell that piece of rock for them?"

"My father, "Ker said. "He had many sheep and sold their fleece; over years, he saved that much."

"Where is he?"

"Dead," Ker said. The dwarf grunted.

"Tell me more. This person gave you a piece of the... the broken stone. And you did what with it?"

Ker told the rest, while the dwarf stared at him out of shiny black eyes.

"You put it under the hearthstone? Near a fire?!" From the tone, that had been the worst place to put the pretty. Ker nodded.

"And then?"

"I had dreams. Bad dreams." The dwarf nodded.

"Yes, yes. It is dangerous, to put such near fire."

"But you said it was just a rock," Ker said. The dwarf grunted again; Ker saw his boots shift a little on the ground. "I don't understand," Ker said. "I mean, I understand that if it belongs to you—to the rockfolk—then you must have it back. But why is it dangerous to put it under a hearthstone?"

"You ask too much," the dwarf said. He looked at the others, and began talking in a language Ker had never heard before. Soon they were arguing—or so it sounded—waving their arms and stamping their feet. Ker wondered if he and his mother might escape unnoticed, and glanced across at her, but she was sitting slumped, her head in her hands. The argument died down, finally, and the dwarf who had been talking to him turned to him again.

"You have a problem," the dwarf said. "It is that you have the scent of... of what we seek about you. And you travel on the Way. And you have *nedross* words."

"*Nedross?*"

"Rock is *dross* or *nedross*. *Dross* does not crumble; it is rock to trust, grain pure throughout. *Nedross* rock cannot be trusted, even if it look solid and pure in grain: it fails. It is—" he paused, searching, "not truth."

Ker felt this as another blow. "I am not lying," he said.

"The words you speak are not whole," the dwarf said. "You know more you do not say."

His mother shifted slightly; the dwarf holding her said something that sounded like rocks grinding and the one facing Ker nodded. Then he spoke again to Ker.

"This is who to you?"

"My mother," Ker said. Did the rockfolk have mothers? Would he understand at all what mothers were to humans?

"Mother is one who birthed you?"

"Yes." Much more than that, but that was the beginning.

The dwarf left Ker abruptly to the hold of the others and went to his mother. Ker started to move, but the ones holding him tightened their grip. It was like being held by rock.

"No smell of dragonspawn," the dwarf said, facing Ker's mother. His hands were clasped behind his back, near the handle of the dagger thrust through his belt. His voice was slightly softer, speaking to her. "You never touched this thing... but you know something. What do you know?"

"I don't know what you speak of," Ker's mother said. "I saw a pretty piece of crystal that Tam said he had given Ker, and he wanted it back."

"Tam. Tam is this one who picked up the stone and broke it?

Tam is where?"

"In the vill—the village you call it. Ravenfield, we say." Ker's mother said. Her face, across the fire, was patched with moving light and shadow. Ker could not read her expression. Her voice sounded tense, even angry. "He is an important man in the village, is Tam Gerisson. And he drove us out—drove us out for nothing. For nothing, I say!"

"Your son did not say that." The dwarf looked back at Ker, scowling. "I said you were not telling all you knew." Then again, to his mother, "Whose words are *nedross*, your words or those of your son?"

"Ker is a good boy," she said. "It is not for the young to condemn their elders or to bear tales of them."

The dwarf's clasped hands shifted, the fingers of one spreading and then folding again around the other. He spoke in his language, and a dwarf Ker had not noticed before moved into the firelight carrying wood, and put it on the fire. The fire leapt higher, giving more light. He turned back to Ker's mother.

"So this is why he told us not more of this person Tam? Because in your folk the young must respect the old?"

Ker's mother nodded. "The young are hasty; the young do not understand everything. So they could make trouble, not understanding, and they must not spread tales of wrongdoing, especially not to strangers. The Lady commands peace."

"But you?"

"I am a widow, a mother, and of the same age as Tam Gerisson. I can judge the rightness of my own words, and I can bear the load of shame or sorrow if I misspeak."

"And you say—" the dwarf prompted.

"I say that Tam planted falsely from the beginning. I say he tricked us, lured my son into plighting troth with his daughter, gave false gifts, lied and plotted to fashion an excuse to send me away."

Ker felt his jaw drop in shock. He had never imagined his mother saying anything like this. "No!" he said. His mother ignored him and went on.

"Ker does not know this, but years ago I turned aside Tam's offer of marriage. He was a lightfaring man, I thought, and I married Ker's father instead, for he had been steady in his affection since we were children. Tam must have held anger against me, though he pretended friendship…"

In the brighter light of the fire, her face looked intent, determined.

"Was he selfish, this Tam?" the dwarf asked. "Hungry for power among your people?"

"Not in seeming. We do not esteem selfish men," his mother said.

Ker stirred. The dwarf whipped around as if he had seen that slight movement.

"What is it?"

"Granna Sofi said Tam became an Elder younger than others. He had the knowledge from his travels…" Ker said.

"So he did," Ker's mother said. "I had forgotten. His oldest children were scarce hip-high. It seemed reasonable, though, because he did know so much. He had often advised the Elders."

"And your husband?"

"He tended the sheep of our people," she said. "He died out on the hills in a storm. He fell and hit his head on a rock."

"Tam had just become an Elder," Ker said. If his mother was telling all about Tam, he had no reason not to tell what he remembered. "He came to tell us the news, and he offered friendship. He said I would be like a son to him, and he a father to me."

"He said he would not hold against me that earlier refusal," Ker's mother said. "He said he would care for me as for a sister. After that, he taught Ker as his own son, in the lore of field and woods."

"Not sheep?" the dwarf asked.

"He was not good with animals," Ker's mother said. "He did not like them, nor they him. Barin Torisson took over the village sheep herd, and Ker learned the arts of planting and harvest. I gave his father's shepherd's crook to Barin, for an extra share of wool."

"And for this Tam gave what?"

"We shared the village harvest. Tam never failed to bring our full measure of grain." Ker saw the sparkle of tears in his mother's eyes, and her head drooped suddenly. "He must have held that anger close, so long… I was afraid, at first, but then all seemed well, until Ker and Tam's daughter saw each other."

"Saw—?"

"As man and woman, not child and child, sister and brother," his mother explained. Ker had not thought about Lin for hours, in the shock of leaving. Now he let his mind wander back to those first hours in which he had seen her truly, not as one of the gaggle of village girls, not as Tam's daughter, but as herself. An individual. A person someone might desire and marry and live with. Suddenly she had seemed wreathed in light, set apart from the others. And on that same day, she had looked at him, recognized him as himself. While he still stood, staring, amazed at what was happening, she had spoken his name, Ker, and it had reverberated through his whole body.

Everyone knew marriage meant joining a family, a lineage, an inheritance of body and mind and soul. But beyond that was the delight of a pairing that worked—fit neatly in all respects as in body. Mere liking was never enough—for as the Elders said, in the spring of youth all maids liked all men and all men liked all maids—but desired in addition to the other criteria.

"The flower of love is the children thereof, but the fruit is peace, harmony, contentment in the whole village," his mother said to the dwarf, as she had told him often. A good marriage enriched everyone; a bad marriage impoverished everyone with the tensions it brought.

"Dwarflove is not like that." The dwarf grinned suddenly, showing those square yellowish pegs. "It is that we find grain match, and of gems those most desired. Dwarflove is blending of the rock, as when fire mountains melt rock into liquid fire."

Ker could not imagine that. The blending he understood was root into soil, or water into root: the growth of green things, flower and fruit.

"But no matter," the dwarf said. It was as if he had never grinned. "It is not the time to speak of love, but of judgment and justice. It is our saying that you go to this man, this Tam Gerisson, and bring back those things of which we spoke, with or without his consent. Bring him also, if you can."

Ker felt a cold gripe in his belly. "I can't," he said. "We were banished. If I return, they will kill me. What good will that do?"

"If you do not return and fulfill this task," the dwarf said. "*We* will kill you." He fingered the axe handle in his belt.

"It is your rock," Ker said. "Why can you not get it for yourself, now that you know where it is?"

The dwarf glowered, then shook his head. "You humans! You know nothing of the matter, and yet you will give orders. The Singers say we are hasty, and men say we are greedy, but in all the world none are so hasty and greedy as humans."

"I didn't say—"

"Be quiet." The dwarf's expression stopped the words in Ker's throat. He sat as still as he could, stone-still, and waited. Finally the dwarf heaved a gusty sigh, and shook his head. "It is not good for the Elders to mingle with humankind, so our wisest say. For where there is no mingling of blood in families, there comes mingling of blood in battle, and we would not begin a war without cause. For this reason, we ask humans to deal with humans, when needs must."

"But why? What is the need? And why didn't those other dwarves just come into the village and talk to Tam? Why did they vanish when he came near?"

"Were you not listening? Have you stones in your ears? You had seen them already: one human already, and I misdoubt they knew you were there until you rose from the water. We are not suited to seeing in water, we rockfolk. So one had seen, but there was no need for two to see. And you had the scent of dragon-spawn on you—"

"Dragonspawn... you said that before, but you said rocks—"

The dwarf muttered what must have been a curse, from the tone. "The scent of what we seek, I mean. Have you no words that mean different things—is there not a food you call dragoncake?"

"Yes..." Ker remembered the village dragoncake, centerpiece of Midwinter Feast. "But—I was in the water. Water washes off scent—"

"Not this scent, not to our noses. Touch it but once, and you bear that scent to the end of your days. Faint, yes, if it is but once, and yet it marks the one who touches it forever."

Ker shuddered. The dwarf nodded.

"You see, now, why this matters. It is worse than that, for the one who handles such carelessly for long, and someone who desires many… they are ill luck for those who do not know how to master them."

"I thought at first," Ker said, "that it was some kind of egg. That it might hatch—" Even now he wouldn't mention Tam's comment about dwarfwives laying eggs.

"Men!" The dwarf spat into the fire, and a green flame shot up. "Can you do nothing but think of that which should not be spoken and bellow it aloud? Be quiet, now."

Again Ker sat silently while the dwarf paced back and forth between him and the fire.

"It is ill, very ill, to speak of some things outside the fortresses of stone," the dwarf said finally. His voice was softer, still gruff but almost pleading. "It will be worse for you and your mother and every one of us, if the wrong ears hear certain things, or the wind carries the tale to certain lands I will not name. You must trust me in this. In time, perhaps, you will know of what I dare not speak. Now—now you must retrieve those stones, to the last splinter, and bring them to us, before… before trouble comes."

"They *were* eggs, weren't they?" Ker said, hardly above a breath in loudness.

The dwarf threw up his hands. "O powers of earth! Save me from this insanity!" He leaned close to Ker then, his strong-smelling breath hot on Ker's face, and murmured into his ear. "Yes, fool, they are eggs. Dragon's eggs. And full of dragonspawn, as your dreams tried to convey. Every crystal splinter holds one, and every unbroken splinter can transform into a dragon if nothing stops it. A hundred, two hundred, a thousand dragons from one egg, do you understand? Those eggs were a thousand and three years old, given into the care of my great-great-uncle straight from the mouth of the dragon himself—"

"Males lay eggs?" Ker asked in a normal voice, forgetting in his curiosity the need for quiet. Quick as a snake's tongue, the dwarf clouted him across the head. He had his dagger in his other hand; he had moved so quickly Ker had not seen him draw it.

"Fool! Idiot! Be quiet before you get us all killed." He sat back on his heels, then twisted to look at Ker's mother. "Madam, speak to your son! If you have any of the proper powers of a mother make him be silent—"

"Ker, please," his mother said. "Please just listen."

Ker nodded, and the dwarf heaved another sigh before going on. "We must be more careful," he said. In his own tongue he spoke to the others, and three of the dwarves trotted away from the fire, up toward the trail. Then he turned back to Ker. "Man, if you try to run I will kill you myself with great gladness and your mother's heart will be reft in twain."

"I will not run," Ker said. "I would not leave her."

"Thanks be for that," the dwarf said. The dwarves holding Ker let go his arms and walked away; he could not hear their footsteps, and once they passed beyond the bright firelight, they disappeared into the darkness. The remaining dwarf watched Ker, and ran his thumb along the side of his dagger with an unmistakable intent. For a time there was no sound but the crackle and hiss of the fire as it burnt lower, and then the dwarf spoke in a low voice.

"It is a trust, a trust between the firefolk of the mountains and my folk of the rocks. No land could sustain all the firefolk that might be born, if they all came hatchlings from the egg, and nothing now in the world can prey upon the great ones, do you understand?"

Ker nodded without speaking. He did not understand what the dwarf meant by all this, but he did understand that the dwarf's patience had worn to nothing, and the dagger blade, naked in the dwarf's hand, glinted in the light that ran blood-red along it.

"For ages of ages, we rockfolk have had this trust, and for ages of ages the firefolk have not numbered more than the land could sustain. Some say of us—the Treesingers would say of us—that we and the firefolk are one in powerlust and greed, but this is not so. The hatchlings, aye: the young of every race are hasty and quick to grab and snatch. Human younglings, I have no doubt, run about and take more than they can use." He turned back to Ker's mother. "Is it not so, mother of a man?"

"It is so," she said.

"Age brings long sight and steady thought," the dwarf said. "The firefolk live long—even longer than we rockfolk, as long as the windfolk perhaps—and the firefolk in their age hold mountains in their care, mountains and valleys and the lands around. They have no wish to despoil what they love."

Ker opened his mouth to say what he knew of dragonkind, but the look on the dwarf's face stopped him. He wanted to say: But they are wicked, greedy, vicious; they are misers who heap up stolen treasure; they prey on travelers. Like dwarves. He did not say it.

"Long ago they made pacts with us rockfolk, for we know the ways of stone as they know the ways of fire, and between us great magics wrought protection for both their younglings and the world. Stone only can stand against such fire; only rockfolk can withstand the pressure of their desire to be free. They enter the bodies of those who touch them, bringing the fire of their ancestors but no wisdom, for they are young and full of foolish ambition. They grow, feeding on their host's body and spirit, until the host is consumed and all but dragonet itself: greedy for power and wealth, proud and lustful."

"I had dreams," Ker said. "Something trapped in the crystal.

When I woke up, I saw a blue flame, a shape, dancing, and then the banked coals went cold."

"And you touched it with bare hands—"

"It felt cold."

"It found no host in you. Perhaps in truth you are *drossin*, as the rockfolk are, for the spawn cannot take a *drossin* host without its consent. Yet from what you say, one or more found a host in this Tam. You say his face was red, and his touch hot: this is indeed the way humankind reacts when filled with dragonspawn."

"So it's… eating him?" Ker's gut twisted as he thought of it—would it be like maggots that sometimes infested the sheep?

"Not exactly. Changing him. When it's grown as far as that host permits, it moves to another. To another of the same household, often. This man has many children?"

"It would go into *children?*"

"Indeed. For it takes time and more time to mature to its next stage."

Lin. Whatever was in Tam would get into Lin, would consume her, change her. Ker forgot his earlier concern, that she had inherited her father's clenched fist. It was not Tam; it was the dragonspawn inside him, and Lin—he could think only of Lin, his Lin, corrupted and consumed by dragonspawn.

"I have to go," he said abruptly, and stood. The dwarf swung a massive fist and knocked him down with a blow to the chest.

"Stay. I am not finished."

"You want me to go. I want to go." Ker could feel his heart pounding. "I have to save her—"

"Save who?"

"Lin. My—Tam's daughter—the girl I was to marry—"

"Ker, no!" That was his mother, across the fire. "She may already—"

"It doesn't matter. I have to—"

"You have to find and return the stones and fragments," the dwarf said. "That is what you must do. Anyone already harboring a dragonspawn is beyond your power. Only a dragon can deal with such a one."

"But if she isn't—" Ker could hear his voice rising like a girl's.

"Take her away, if you can. But I do not think you can." The dwarf shook his head.

"If they do not kill me first, I will," Ker said.

"If you rush in to save a girl, they will kill you," the dwarf said. His voice now held amusement. "By Sertig's hammer, I find myself where you were but an hour agone. You cannot go without being killed—not in this mood—so you must not go until you see sense."

"I won't rush in," Ker said. "I'll be careful."

"And why do you now think being careful will work, while before you did not?"

Ker could not answer that, but an idea came to him. "If you would show me how to do that—what the others did—to not be seen, then I could get in and out and no one would know."

"It is not something for humans to learn," the dwarf said. "It is born in us. But perhaps we can help without that." He pulled from his pocket a grey cloth about the size his mother draped over the dough trough. "This is not a way to be unseen, but a way to be unnoticed, if someone moves quietly and quickly. I do not know if it will work on you, but we shall see."

He draped it on Ker's head; for an instant the fire seemed to blur, then his vision cleared. The dwarf leaned close. "Get up and walk around the fire, very quietly, until you are near your mother. Say nothing. When you are beside her, speak to her."

Ker stood; he was stiff from sitting so long, but he moved

as quietly as possible. When he looked at his mother, she was looking where he had been, not at him. He spoke, then, and her head turned sharply. "Ker! I didn't see you move! Are you leaving, then?"

"Yes—very soon, now." He looked back at the dwarf.

"It is only deception, and not as strong on you as on us; I could see you easily. But then, I knew about it. Stay close to hedges and thickets, cast no shadows into someone's eyes, and you may pass unseen." Or may not, the dwarf's expression said. "Rest a little," the dwarf said. "You will need your rest." That, as if he and his fellows had not broken Ker's sleep in the first place. But under that commanding gaze, Ker lay down. When the dwarf shook him awake, dawn was grey to the east. "You had better go now," the dwarf said. "Take this—" He handed Ker a flattened lump. "It is food and will give you strength. And whatever you do, do not trust one who might have the dragonspawn already, no matter who it is."

The journey back went swiftly, for it was mostly downhill and Ker had no burden to carry. The dwarf's food brought him fully awake with the first bite and lent speed to his feet.

He moved cautiously as he came into the vill's pasturelands.

No one watched the cattle grazing in the upper pasture; Ker knew where the herdsmen rested, and no herdsmen lay there. No one watched the sheep in their meadow; half had strayed into the hedge where the rustvine grew, which no shepherd would allow, for the thorns that tangled the fleece. Ker wondered at that, for it meant the shepherd had been away for hours. He took the sheep's path to the stream, to the shelving bank where the sheep drank. Here the water swirled in, clean and clear, but there was no ford, and no path on the far side.

The water cooled his feet, and he waded upstream to the women's bathing pool, alert for voices, half-hoping he would find Lin bathing alone and could speak to her. No voices. He came out into a little glade, the grass dry underfoot, and followed the women's path back to the village. He saw no one, heard no one, until he was very close, close enough to see through the fringe of vines at the wood's edge. The blackened ruin of his mother's house, burnt to ash and scorched stone hearth, lay between him and the rest of the village. It still stank of the burning.

Now he could hear voices, many voices and one angry voice louder than them all. He could see Tam in the middle of the square, yelling, and the other adults talking. The men should have been in the fields at this time of day, and the woman in houses and gardens, or at the well, but all the people seemed to be there, milling about. Ker watched, trying to hear what they said, but he could not. He wondered what had happened.

"You have to!" Tam yelled louder than before. "I know more! I have power!" He raised a fist.

Ker edged around one house and then another, working his way toward Tam's. If they were all in the meeting, arguing, perhaps he could get in and out with the eggs before someone saw him. At the corner of Granna Sofi's garden, he looked across at Tam's house. Its only door faced the square, but two windows looked out on this side. He had only to cross the garden with its clusters of pie plant and redroot, and climb in through the window. If no one was inside.

He dared not look to see if Tam's family were all in the square; he was too close. Even with the dwarf's cloth, someone might notice him. He could see safely out of Granna Sofi's windows, though, and she had a back door. He eased through it, blinking as his eyes adjusted to the darker room, pulled off the cloth, and took two steps toward the front of the house before he realized that Granna Sofi was there, staring at him, her mouth open. She lay on a narrow bed, propped on pillows.

"You…" she breathed in her quavery old woman's voice.

"Please," Ker said, not even sure what he was asking. Don't raise an alarm. Don't be afraid. Don't turn your back on me.

"You came back," she said. Her voice rasped.

"Yes. I have to do something."

"You said something was wrong with Tam," she said. He looked more closely at her and saw that something was wrong with her, with the way she lay, with the shape of her legs and the color of her skin.

"Granna Sofi—what is it?"

"You were right," she said. "He has changed. He has become something else."

"I know. I have to stop it."

"You cannot stop it. He will kill you. He killed me because I spoke against him."

"But—" *But you're alive,* he thought, even as her eyes sagged shut and her last breath rattled free of her ribs. He saw then that her legs were broken, that great bruises marred her arms. Ker made the signs to send her spirit away in peace, and looked around for the necessary herbs. There they were, wrapped in a twist of sourgrass, as if the old woman had known she was going to die that day. Perhaps she had. He shivered, and laid the herbs on her eyes and mouth, at her head and feet.

When he looked out her front window, he could see Tam clearly, the red sunburnt face and arms, the fierce expression on his face. He could feel the waves of heat that came off the square. Tam's wife Ila stood beside him, and she too looked ruddy under the sun, her yellow hair blazing with light. Around them at a

112

little distance stood the others of the town, children at the back, peering between the adults.

It must be now. He hurried out Granna Sofi's back door, and quickly stepped across the first row of plants, then the second, and then he was flattened against the wall of Tam's house. He listened a long moment, hearing nothing from within. Tam continued to harangue the villagers from the square. Ker tried not to listen, as he would have tried not to swallow filth, but some words leaked through his ears anyway.

He must do it. He must enter the house as a thief, and as a thief he must steal away Tam's treasure, both the dragon's eggs and the daughter. He turned and climbed in through the low window. As before, his eyes took a moment to adjust to the dimness. He reached for the cloth, to take it off, and realized he'd left it in Granna Sofi's house. He moved aside from the window, and stumbled against a bench, and then in an instant he was wrapped in someone's arms, and a hot mouth pressed against his, and the voice he had long dreamed of said, "Oh... you came back..."

Lin. He freed his mouth and said "Lin. I have to do something—"

"Yes—you have to kiss me. Oh, Ker, I've been so unhappy—" She clung to him and he could feel every sweet curve of her body. They had never been this close; he had dreamed of being this close. "Take me away, Ker; take me away with you! I want you, I want you forever."

He had never imagined that she would choose him over her father's will. He had expected to have to argue with her, persuade her.

"I will," he said. "But first I have to do something. Help me, and then we'll go—"

"No, let's go now," she said, dragging him toward the window.

"No, Lin, it's important—" He pulled back far enough to see her clearly. Lin with her yellow hair inherited from her mother, her clear eyes, her creamy skin… now flushed with passion, with love for him.

"What, then?" she said, clearly impatient. "If Da finds you here, he'll kill you—maybe both of us. We have to go—"

"In a moment. Lin, where does he keep the rock eggs, the ones with the pretties—"

"You're going to steal his pretties?" Her voice rose, then hushed quickly, and she grinned at him. "What a sweet vengeance, Ker. I hardly dared think you could think of that—"

"Under the hearthstone?" he asked, turning toward it. The dwarf had told him he would feel the pull of the dragonspawn, but all he felt now was Lin's nearness and his own body's response.

"Some of them," she said. "But not all—" And with a gesture very unlike the girl he'd known, she pulled open her bodice to show him the purplish crystal spike hung from a thong about her neck, nestling between her breasts. His heart faltered, then raced.

"Lin, no! Take it off! It will hurt you!"

"Take it off? I will not! Da gave it me, to make up for sending you away. It's the one you had; I'll never take it off."

"But Lin, they're dangerous!"

"Ker, don't be silly. It's a rock, a pretty rock. How can it be dangerous? The only dangerous thing here is Da, if he finds us. Here—I'll show you the others—" And she lifted the massive hearthstone as easily as Ker would have lifted a hoe, and scooped up two whole egg-shaped rocks, and a handful of shards. "This should be enough."

"We have to get them all," Ker said, and his own voice sounded strange to him. Where had Tam found another egg? He looked around and took a cloth from a hook near the fireplace.

"Here—put them in this. We shouldn't touch them."

"They don't burn," Lin said, but she gave him what she held, then reached down for the other shards. As she did, the banked fire went out with a last hiss, and Ker saw the glow of her skin against the dark hole, and all at once her hand seemed clawlike, the nails talons. When she looked up at him, his stomach clenched at the expression on her face… exultant, hungry, eager…

"Is that all?" Ker asked. "Are you sure?"

"My father was right," Lin said with a giggle that froze his heart. "You are a greedy thief, aren't you?"

He could say nothing. He was robbing her father, though it was not greed, and he had no way to explain it. Not to the girl whose skin shone in the dim room. He wanted to tell her everything, but the dwarf's final warning stopped his tongue. That and his fear.

"Come now," Lin said, moving to the window. "I don't mind if you're greedy. I'm used to that in a man. I know you'll provide for me—"

"Lin—" What could he say? What he had most feared had happened already; he could not prevent it; he had come too late. He could not go with her, wherever she was going; he could not stay here.

"Come *on*, Ker," she said, reaching back to grasp his arm and tug at him. "We need to leave now. We can find a place later, and—"

He moved, hardly aware of moving, following her out through the window, across the garden again, behind Granna Sofi's house toward the next garden, the next house. Behind them the crowd in the square gave a concerted gasp. Lin did not look around, but Ker did.

Above the square hung a shadow of light, light condensed

into form, form overwhelming light. The shape writhed, growing until it filled the air above the square, brightening more and more. Ker paused, terrified but fascinated. What could it be? What was Tam doing? Beneath that light, Tam looked up, and the other villagers edged away, pushing at the children behind them.

"Ker!" Lin's voice, from the edge of the village, near the ashes of what had been his house. "Come quickly! Before Da sees us!"

Light squirmed in the air; shifting colors flowed over the crowd, then faded. Tam's face paled; his mouth opened; his hands spread, as if to push the light away. Heat pressed down, heavy, inexorable. Something crackled; Ker looked across the crowd and saw a ribbon of flame leap up the thatch of Othrin's house and spread. Those nearest turned, opened their mouths to shout a warning. With a roar, two other houses burst into flame, then a third. People screamed; Ker could see their mouths open, but only the roar of the fires sounded in his ears.

Pain stung his hands. He looked down and saw the cloth wrapping of his burden browning like toast over coals.

He ran. He ran without thought, without plan, away from the heat, away from the light, straight into the woods on no path at all, blundering into trees and stumbling over briars, until he fell headlong into the stream. Steam hissed away from his burden; the blackened cloth fell to pieces. His hands opened; water flowed between his fingers, cooling, soothing. Under the water, he could see the stones: two whole, one broken, a heap of shards.

Behind him in the village, fire raged; he could hear the roar, the crackling; he could hear screams. Acrid smoke spread through the trees. Overhead, thunder boomed in the cloudless sky; lighter light departed. Shaking, Ker got to his feet in the shallow water, took off his shirt, and wrapped his scorched hands, then fished the stones and pieces out of the slow current and waded down-stream to look for a place to climb out.

When he came around a turn of the stream, Lin stood on the ford, waiting for him. She looked flushed and lovely, her hair curling around her shoulders, her body the shape of every man's dream. She smiled at him.

"We don't have to worry about Da now," she said. "We can go back. You can be an Elder—"

"No," Ker said.

"Well, then, we can go somewhere else. With Da's pretties, we'll have enough to start a new place—" A little breeze blew a lock of shining hair across her face; she tossed it back, the gesture he remembered from their childhood.

"No," Ker said.

"You're not running away," she said. The smile changed, reshaped into a mask of anger. "Don't think you can take what's mine and run away from me, leave me again!" Her hand reached for the crystal she wore, and he could see in her all that he had seen in her father. "Give them back, then, thief!"

The words echoed, throbbing in air that once again thickened into light incarnate. He had a momentary image of Lin consumed in light, rising into its maw.

She was gone. The strange light was gone. On the ford stood a man dressed in such finery as Ker had never seen or imagined: brilliant colors, glossy fabrics, feathers and lace... he did not even have the words to say what he saw. The man stood in a shaft of brilliant sunlight that pierced the overarching trees, and the smoke filtering through the trees flowed around him.

"I believe," the man said, "you have something of mine."

Ker tightened his grip on his bundle. "It belongs to the rock-folk," Ker said. "I do not know you."

"To the rockfolk." A dry chuckle, thornbush scraping on stone. "I suppose that is one way of saying it. Are you then returning it, or are you the thief she called you?"

"I am not a thief," Ker said. "I am taking it back to them."

The man stared at him, until Ker coughed on the smoke blowing through the trees, and then the man shrugged and blew away, as if he had been smoke himself. Ker struggled out of the water, and made his way up the trail, coughing now and then as the smoke eddied past him.

Over the first rise, the same man stood by the path, leaning on a tree. "You might fare better if you had a horse," he said.

"I have never had a horse," Ker said.

"A walking stick, then," the man said, and held out a trimmed length of wood with the bark still on. "You have a long way to go."

"It is ill luck to take gifts of strangers," Ker said.

"It is ill luck to refuse gifts of dragons," the man said, and as before he blew away... but this time into the thickening of light, which condensed into a shape the size of a hill. Green as the man's coat on the back, and yellow as the man's shirt underneath, clothed in shining scales that shimmered from one color to another. Ker gulped, swallowed, and stood still.

"Mortals," said the dragon. The dragon was not looking at Ker, but up into the air, as if talking to it.

Ker took a step forward, up the trail, and the dragon's great eye rolled toward him. He stopped.

"You interest me," the dragon said. A long flame-colored tongue flicked out of its mouth and touched Ker on the forehead; he felt it as a bee-sting, hot and then sore. "I taste my children on you, but not in you. I taste dwarf on you. Perhaps you tell the truth?"

"I—I am," Ker said. Sweat rolled down his face; heat came off the dragon as off a rock wall on which the sun has lain all day. "They sent me to bring these back—" He shifted the burden in his hands.

"It is… difficult," the dragon said. "They do belong… there." The dragon sighed, and the grass before it withered and turned brown at the edges. For a moment, the dragon's eye looked down its snout, then it lifted its head. "Lowland life is so fragile," it said, as if to itself. Then to Ker: "Approach me."

With the dragon's eye on him, he could not disobey. He took one step after another, until the heat beat against his face and body.

"What do your people say of dragons?" the dragon asked.

It was impossible to lie. "My people say dragons are wise," Ker said. "And greedy, treacherous, and cruel."

"My people say humans are stupid," the dragon said. "And greedy, treacherous, and cruel. Which is better, if one must be cruel: stupid and cruel or wise and cruel?"

In the worst of the nightmares, Ker had never dreamt of holding a conversation with a dragon. "Wisdom is good," he said, trying for caution.

"Wisdom alone is useless," the dragon said. "Wisdom without power is wind without air… it can do nothing of itself." Ker said nothing; he could think of nothing to say. The dragon twitched its head. "And power without wisdom is fatal. Power without wisdom is a mad bull running through the house." The dragon focused both eyes on Ker. "A fool should have no power, lest he bring ruin with him, but a wise man must have power, lest his wisdom die without issue. So which are you, mortal: fool or wise man?"

Something more than his own life hung on his answer, Ker

knew, but not what it was. "I try to be good," he said.

The dragon vented flame from its nostrils, over his head. "Good! Evil! Words for children to use. Can fools ever bring good, or true wisdom do evil? No, no, little man. You must choose: are you fool or wise man?"

"Anyone would choose to be wise, but it is not possible to choose," Ker said. "Some are born unable to become wise."

Something rattled off to his right; Ker glanced that way and saw the tip of the dragon's tail slithering across its vast hind leg.

"You interest me again," the dragon said. "So you would choose to be wise if you could be wise?"

"Of course," Ker said.

"And of what does wisdom consist?" the dragon asked.

Ker could think of no answer for that. He knew he was not wise; how then could he know what wisdom was? Finally he said, "Only the wise know."

"Does beauty know what beauty is?" the dragon asked. "Does water know wetness, or stone hardness?" Its head tilted, so that one great eye was higher than the other, and both looked cross-eyed down its snout at Ker. His mouth went even dryer than before. Scaled eyelids slid up over the dragon's eyes for a moment and dropped back down, leaving that penetrating gaze even clearer than before. Ker's stomach twisted; eyelids should not move like that. "Surely not," the dragon said, hissing slightly. "Nor the blue of the sky know its blueness, nor the green of grass its greenness."

A throbbing silence followed; Ker could find nothing to say. He glanced around, trying to think of something, anything, that would free him from the dragon's gaze, and saw that its tail now lay between him and the trail back, a narrow but steep ridge. He was trapped in the dragon's circle.

"I will tell you," the dragon said finally, "what wisdom is, if you will promise to become wise."

"How can I promise that?" Ker blurted in a panic. Sweat ran down his ribs, and dried in the heat of the dragon's breath.

"Small beings can have small wisdom," the dragon said. "And small wise beings are better than small fools. Listen: wisdom is caring for afterwards."

"Caring for afterwards...?" Ker repeated this without understanding.

"After action, afterwards," the dragon said. "Choose the afterwards first, then the action. Fools choose action first."

Ker opened his mouth to say that only fortune-tellers could know what would happen, but fear stopped him: would he really argue with a dragon while trapped in its circle?

The dragon's snout edged closer, nudged him. He staggered back: a dragon's nudge was like a blow from a strong man. Or a dwarf.

"You see," the dragon murmured. "You do know."

He didn't know. He didn't know anything except that he was surrounded by large lumps and ridges of dragon and too afraid to shake or fall down. He closed his eyes, expecting searing flame or rending teeth, and tried to think of the village as it had been, before Tam found those terrible eggs... of Lin before she had been invaded... of his mother, who now waited out on the hills in a hollow with a spring and a handful of rockfolk.

Cool air swirled around him, rose to a gale of dust and leaves, then stilled. He opened his eyes. No dragon. No strange light in the air. He blinked. A streak of dead grass, scorched, where the dragon had breathed that tongue of fire... and new grass, growing quick as a flame, brilliant green against the charred ground. At his feet lay the walking stick he had refused before, now sprouting incongruous flowers and leaves.

Ker looked up and around and saw nothing of the dragon, but he had seen nothing of the dragon before. Cautiously, he picked up the stick in his free hand. At once, strength flowed back into his limbs. He felt rested, strong, as if he had just come from a full night's sleep and a full meal. The scent of those flowers filled his nose. He took a step, and stared as the land blurred around him, reappearing when he put that foot down. A league, two leagues, had fled behind him. Already he could see the hill where his mother waited with the rockfolk.

One more step, and he was there, standing above the dell and looking down into it with eyes that saw through leaves and wood to where his mother sat knitting, while the rockfolk snored. The ones who should have been watching the trail slumped near it, also snoring. The little camp looked orderly and peaceful; someone had put their scattered belongings back into the packs. Probably his mother; he could not imagine the dwarves being so helpful. Somewhere a bird called, and another answered. Ker looked at the walking stick. Flowers and leaves had disappeared, leaving it bark-covered once more.

Ker came carefully down the slope into camp; his mother looked up and her face brightened but she said nothing.

"I'm back," he said.

"What happened?"

He did not know how to tell her; he was not sure exactly what had happened.

"Why are they sleeping?" he asked instead. His mother shrugged.

"I know not. Only that at noon, the light changed, and they all fell into sleep. I would have slept, but their snores were too loud and I was worried... did you bring Lin?"

"No." Ker leaned the walking stick against a tree; the tree's foliage thickened. His mother stared at him.

"What happened? What is that? How did you come so soon?"

"I don't understand," Ker said. "It was a dragon—" He could say no more; exhaustion fell on him like a sack of wet grain, and he slumped to the ground. In a moment, his mother was at his side. A long drink of water, a hunk of bread smeared with jam, and he struggled up again to sit with his back against a tree. She handed him his spare shirt, and he put it on. He tried to tell her everything, but how could he say what he did not understand?

The rockfolk roused suddenly, their snores cut off in an instant. Their eyes opened; they sat up and stared at him.

"Why are you here?" asked the leader. "Why did you come back before you had finished?"

"I brought you what you asked for," Ker said. He nudged the wrapped bundle with his foot.

"You could not have gone so far so fast—" the dwarf broke off, staring now at the bundle. He muttered in his own language, and two of the others approached, one drawing a thick leather bag from his pack and opening its mouth. The first unwrapped the bundle gingerly, and revealed the same egg-shaped rocks, the same shards. He reached out, touched them, turned them over. Then he glared at Ker. "How did you do this?"

"Do what?"

"They're dead. They're all dead. What did you do to them?"

"I did nothing," Ker said. He couldn't see any difference in the rocks and shards, but the dwarves clearly did.

"These can't be the same… you could not have traveled so fast…"

"It was the dragon," Ker said. They all stared at him now. "It—gave me a walking stick. It helped me."

Now they stared at the walking stick, and the thick growth of new leaves on the tree overhead.

"You talked to a dragon and it *helped* you? It brought you eggs to carry?"

"No." His head ached now, sudden as if someone had hit him again. "Let me tell you—"

"Go ahead."

He told it as well as he could and they listened without interruption, though some of them muttered softly in their own tongue. When he finished, with "And then you woke up," the questions began. What was the dragon's name, and how big, and what color, and what had it done with Tam and the villagers and Lin? Ker said "I don't know" over and over.

"You cannot know so little," the dwarf said. "You were there! You say you saw these things, and yet—"

"Don't bully him," his mother said. "You're as bad as Tam, you lot." She glowered at them, and to Ker's surprise they gave way. "What would he know of dragons? Do you think they give their names away to anyone?"

"Rarely," drawled a new voice. Ker twisted around to see the same elegant man lounging on the slope above, a stalk of sweetgrass in his mouth. The dwarves drew into a huddle, eyes wide. The man lifted one shapely eyebrow. "Frightened, stonebrethren? Lost something? It would have been wise, would it not, to have told me before I heard it from others? Before I had to reveal myself, to undo the harm that came from that loss?"

One of the dwarves burst into speech in their tongue, but the man held up a hand. "Be courteous; these human folk have not your language nor mine. Speak as they can hear."

"We weren't sure," the dwarf said. "Not at first. We thought—"

"You hoped you could retrieve what you lost before I learned of it, is that not true?"

"Yes." The dwarf scuffed one boot against another.

"So, this human—this idiot, this fool, I believe you called him—has proved more wise than you, has he not? He, not you, retrieved the lost. You sent him to do it, knowing it was perilous—"

"It was his fault in the first place," muttered one of the dwarves.

"You accuse him of thievery?" the man said. "You think he slit the carrybag and filched the eggs in the first place?"

"Well... no. Probably not." The dwarf looked down, hunching his shoulders.

"You know they seek life," the man said. "My kind always do. Whoever carried them grew careless, I have no doubt: drank deep and slept, as you slept today, or set the carrybag on sharp rock, and so they fell free, to be found by something or someone they could use." He sighed. "I should remember that ages are long for you, stonebrethren, and a trust passed from generation to generation can be a trust weakened."

"We didn't mean—" began the first dwarf, but his voice trailed away as the man looked at him.

"Intentions..." the man said slowly. Then he looked at Ker's mother. "Madam, what does a mother say about intentions?"

"Meaning to never mended a wall," Ker's mother said. "Not meaning to drop it never patched a pitcher."

"So wise a lady," the man said. "This must be your son." Now he looked at Ker, and it seemed that behind his mild brown eyes red flames danced.

"He's a good boy," she said.

"He's an interesting man," the man said, in a tone of mild correction. "He may become wise one day. We shall see." Now he looked at Ker. "What of you? What do you see in all this?"

Ker's throat tightened, but he forced words past the tightness. "You are not a man," he said.

That elegant figure laughed. "True and true: what, then, am I?"

"A dragon."

"Perhaps. Perhaps merely the shape a dragon sends to talk to those who cannot bear the sight of dragons. For if the shape be the thing, then this shape of man cannot be a dragon, nor—" The man was gone; words hung in the air as the light condensed once more and a very visible dragon sprawled on the trail above, its head lying aslant on the slope to the dell. "—Nor can this be a man's shape. But if some essence, not the shape, be the thing, then either the man's shape or some other could be dragon."

"Lord dragon," one of the dwarves said, coming forward past Ker. Ker noticed that he was paler than usual. "If you permit us—"

"I do not," said the dragon. "Be still, rockbrethren; we will talk hereafter." There was in that a chill threat. Ker and the dwarf both shivered, but the dragon was looking at Ker. "You remember we talked of wisdom... what would a wise being say of these who lost somewhat of value held in trust and did not warn the owner that it was lost?"

"You ask me to judge them?" Ker said. He glanced at the dwarves, now standing motionless as if the command to be still had turned them to stone.

"I ask your opinion only," the dragon said. "I am capable of judgment; it is my gift."

"I do not know the ways of rockfolk," Ker began. The dragon's eye kindled, and he went on hastily. "But these had cause to hate and distrust us—me and my mother—and instead they listened and did not harm us."

126

"You bear their bruises on your face," the dragon commented.

Ker shrugged. "I bear them no malice for it," he said. "They were frightened; they thought I might have stolen those things they sought, and that danger would come of it."

"They sent you into danger," the dragon said.

"Yes, but—" The dwarves' reasons now seemed like excuses, as he'd first thought. Even so he wanted no part of vengeance. "They did not force me; when I thought of Lin I wanted to go."

"To save a friend."

More than a friend, but he did not think the dragon would care for a correction. "Yes. And these dwarves were trying to make right what had gone wrong. They wanted to restore what was lost. I think they are honest, but too frightened—of you, I suppose—"

"Oh, yes, I am frightening…" The dragon rolled its head and inspected its own length. A cloud of steam gushed from its mouth, warm and moist, smelling of baked apples. "And so fear is their excuse, is that what you would say? But you… you were not frightened enough to give me what you were not sure was mine. Are you then braver than the rockbrethren?"

"No," Ker said instantly. "I'm—I was scared. I am scared. But I had to do it anyway."

"Hmmmm." That vibrated in the rocks beneath their feet; the trees trembled. "So, you make no judgment against them for the harm they did to you, by loosing such dangers on you and your people, and then by striking you, and then by sending you into danger?"

"I am not the judge," Ker said. The dragon's eyelids flipped up and back down again, and again Ker felt sick at his stomach.

"You are more clever than you seemed at first. Remember what wisdom is?"

"Care for afterwards," Ker recited promptly.

"Yes… and have you a care for afterwards here? What about their afterwards?"

Ker looked at the dwarves. They all looked at him with an expression of resigned defeat.

"If I were the judge," Ker said, "I would do no more than has already happened. They have been afraid to the marrow of their bones; they have suffered enough. "

"Would you trust them again?" the dragon asked, cocking its head to peer closely at Ker out of one eye.

"I would," Ker said. His back felt cold; he glanced around to see that the fire had died down to glowing embers.

"Why?"

Ker shrugged. "I don't know. They feel honest to me."

"So in *their* afterwards they prosper as the result of their carelessness… will this make them less careless?" The dragon had propped its chin on one vast front claw.

"I do not know," Ker said. "You asked what I thought."

"So." The dragon's head lifted a little, and the warmth of its breath touched Ker. "Hear my judgment, rockbrethren. For your carelessness in a sworn trust, you shall lose the gems in these—" A lance of flame, accurate as a pointing finger, touched the rocks and shards; Ker hardly felt warmth as it struck past him. When he turned to look, the rocks and shards had vanished. "Yet I will trust that you continue to guard the others well, and make no demands of reparation. So tell your king. I will watch more closely, but that is all. And I will also watch how you deal with this human, whom you have to thank for my inclination to mercy."

The dwarves threw themselves on the ground; the dragon withdrew into the fastnesses of air. They looked up when it had gone, and scrambled to their feet.

"We've you to thank," their leader said. His mouth twisted, then he smiled. "Well, that's fair, I suppose. And what do you want of us, then?"

"N-nothing," Ker said. His knees felt shaky again.

"That won't do," the dwarf said. "Sertig knows we're not as rulebound as our cousins of the Law, but no one can say the brothers are mean enough to take such a service as you did us and give no gifts in return. And it's not for the dragon's sake, either," he said, glaring up at the leaf canopy overhead. "I need no dragon to teach me generosity." A bubble of light rippled through the dell, and he paled, but shook his head. "No, and again no. We're in your debt, a debt we can't pay, but we can gift you with what we have." He looked around at the others. "Come now, lads, let's get busy."

Before Ker quite realized what they were about, the dwarves had picked up the bundles he and his mother had carried from the village the day before.

"Where was it you were going, ma'am?" he asked Ker's mother.

"I—I have family in the hills west of here," she said. "Swallowbank…"

"Swallowbank, yes. A difficult road, ma'am, and a hard three days' journey, if you'll pardon my saying so. Would you consent to travel an easier one?"

"I—" she looked at Ker. "I—I suppose so. What road?"

"Ours," the dwarf said. He turned to Ker. "We will take you on our road, smooth and straight and safe underfoot and over-head, we will carry all your burdens, and we will set you down safe and rested in sight of Swallowbank with all that you desire," he said. "If you will accept our gift."

"I   thought—maybe—with   Tam   gone,   and   the

dragonspawn—we could go back," Ker said. "Rebuild our village—" Surely they were not all dead, all the people he had known; surely the dragon would not have killed them all.

The dwarf shook his head. "No. I'm sorry, but what the dragon deals with cannot be changed. For all they are great healers in their way, they are also great destroyers. That land will not accept humans for a span of years; the dragon would have made sure of that. You must find a new place, and a new life."

"Then—I accept your offer with thanks." Ker picked up the walking stick, half-expecting to be dragged a league away with his first step, but it remained a bark-covered stick.

The dwarf led them back up the way Ker had come down with firewood, to a rock face smoothed by falling water. The rock opened suddenly, like a door, and they passed into a dark tunnel, smooth all around. At once, the walking stick burst into cold flame, lighting the tunnel in blue radiance. Ker stared at it, but it did not burn his hand, so he held it firmly and walked on.

Author's Note on "Final Honor"

In *Deeds of Youth*, "Mercenary's Honor" first published in *Operation Arcana*, introduced Ilanz Balentos, a one-eyed mercenary commander in late middle age hoping to set up as a ruler of a small domain, Aliam Halveric in his early years as a mercenary commander from Lyonya, and Halveric's then-squire, Kieri. Now it's seven years later than the end of that story. Ilanz is almost completely blind and Aliam brings bad news. In terms of Paksworld history, we've leapt a few thousand years and the Immerhoft Sea to Margay in Aarenis. Still in the past but much closer to Paksenarrion's birth. Kieri doesn't appear in this story (Aliam has sent him to be trained for knighthood in the Company of Falk), but someone else known to readers of the first Paksworld stories does: Aesil M'dierra, Balentos' young niece, who will become owner and commander of Golden Company a few years hence, has recently been names Balentos' heir.

Publication Note: "Final Honor" is new, written exclusively for *Deeds of Wisdom*.

FINAL HONOR

Ilanz Balentos stood by the window of his office, staring out. He saw only a narrowing blur of golds and oranges: fall flowers around a field already plowed and sown for winter wheat, the dark soil almost as dark as the rest of his vision. He had hoped to have ten years before his good eye failed this far. He'd had seven. Seven years of mostly peace, time to grow a row of fruit trees and fragrant roses in his garden.

Time for his small realm to thrive.

Not time, however, to wear out the enmity of Vonja or eliminate the ambition of Sorellin. Vonja wanted Margay destroyed, and the Count of Margay, Ilanz himself, dead. Sorellin wanted the rich fields that lay on Sorellin's side of the town.

"I'm sorry, Ilanz, to bring such ill news."

Aliam Halveric, one of his captains, and his squire had arrived that afternoon. "But you must tell her; the danger is here, and growing every day. You must get out while there's time."

His guests had brought the worst of news. Alliance between Vonja and Sorellin. Their combined military force far outweighed what he had... what he could gather.

His hopes, Ilanz realized, had fooled his judgment.

He had fooled the people he led, the people he protected.

Far from their savior, he was their destroyer. And his niece... that bold young woman, the girl who wanted to be what he had been, a soldier, a mercenary commander—what would come of her dreams?

He turned back to the room, so dim his sight he could see only the flames of the lamps. He knew every distance in the room, could walk about as if sighted, and came back to his own chair, hardly needing to touch it as he sat down.

"We can get you both out safely, in disguise," Halveric said. "We can do that on the way out, and we can carry some coin for her. You know I will watch out for her."

Halveric's face, close to the table lamp, was a reddish blur. It vanished again as Halveric leaned back. "I wish I could take all your men, and your people too, but we would be seen and attacked, and my only way to get here was in disguise." A short pause, in which Ilanz said nothing because he was too choked with guilt and shame. "It would be best to leave tonight, with you and her and perhaps a handful more. Safer for her."

It would not be safer, Ilanz thought, because Aesil would refuse to sneak off, leave the others unprotected. She had left a home of wealth and power—her father was a witward of Pliuni—and traveled alone through robber-ridden wilds to Valdaire, to join his Company. She had survived her early mistakes to become one of his captains and his heir.

She would want to stay and fight.

He'd hoped—with a younger, healthier, sighted com-mander—that his troops would be enough to keep Margay safe, and she would be safe, and he could relax and die in peace. But Halveric's warning stripped away that illusion. What could he give her to live on if she left now? Only too much gold to carry easily, most of it still in his bank in Valdaire.

"She won't want to go," he said to Halveric. "She wants to soldier, and she's good at it."

"I'll take her for a while," Halveric said. "I didn't do that bad with Kieri. But if she's ambitious…"

"She expects to inherit my place," Ilanz said. "I told her; I told my captains. She's a natural leader as well as a natural fighter. But what you say—"

"It's not possible." Halveric's face moved back into the light. His voice held compassion but no hope that a sighted commander would be able to hold Margay together. "They have four outposts around Margay now, close enough to coordinate an attack together, close enough to one another that it would be impossible to move even a half-cohort between them without being seen and attacked. A larger force might fight free, but Vonja lies between here and the Guild Road to Valdaire, and Sorellin lies between you and the Guild Road to the north. The whole company could not use the Guild League road back to Valdaire without losing half or more. It might make it across country to Cortes Cilwan, but Cilwan might attack, not knowing if it was truly hostile or coming for asylum. Speaking of which—"

"Asylum?"

"Andressat will take you in."

"You asked him?" Ilanz knew he sounded angry.

"Ilanz, I had to do something… so, yes, I asked. And the Count said he would take you, your niece, and a hand of followers but could not take more."

"You'll stay while I tell her?"

"Of course. Maybe she'll have some ideas too."

Ilanz heard her quick steps on the stairs, lighter than his other captains'.

"Here, my lord," she said when she reached his office, in

proper form before any visitor, even known ones. He was "Uncle Ilanz" only when they were alone.

"Lord Halveric has brought me a puzzle of sorts," Ilanz said. "Take a look at the map he brought."

He hadn't been able to see it clearly; Aesil's eyesight was excellent, he knew. Her blurred shape leaned over the table. And as usual these days, she told him what she was seeing without referencing his blindness.

"Yes, my lord. I recognize the Guild League road, and there's Pler Vonja and Sorellin. The little road over to Hijou Vonja. But there's a rectangle on one corner of the sheet. I don't know what it is—"

"That rectangle," Halveric said. "It's an outpost that could house two hundred men and supplies for a quarter-year. Underground. If it were aboveground, it would clearly be a military camp. Out of sight of the Guild League road and your bounds. It caught my squire's attention because these straight lines are deep ditches; he wondered who was ditching a slanted field. It's planted above, grass and bushes, but the plantings show the building lines, at least in this season."

"How many troops are there?" Ilanz asked.

"None now," Halveric's captain said. "Except a tensquad, to keep people like me away. They're pretending to herd about four sheep." He grinned. "Squire Bellorn warned me, so I wasn't seen. I got right into one ditch and into what they're hiding. It's like a town of cellars with footed stone walls, all roofed with sod and other plants. Could later be built up, with what's there as cellars. An odd sort of town. It has mostly long, narrow rooms that front the ditches, but some are larger, built farther in, and those contain supplies—grain, cloth, leather, and weapons. Construction must have started at least a year back, maybe more."

"Weapons!"

"Yes, my lord. Pikes and swords, mostly."

Ilanz grunted. "So—they've moved in supplies—"

"But no one's there," Aesil said. "Are they?"

"They will bring them in, traveling light and fast," Ilanz said. He turned to Halveric. "Two hundred, you say? They will have more than two hundred…"

Halveric shifted in his seat; Ilanz heard, and looked over at him.

"Yes, Aliam?"

"We came the long way 'round, as I said. Through Sorellin. They've also built similar things. We found four; they might have more. And theirs might serve for a war against Vonja as well as Margay."

"Each garrisoned with two hundred. But those two have quarreled before; maybe their treaty won't hold."

"From what I heard—on my own and by spies—it will hold through the attack." Halveric leaned forward again. "And I'm afraid it may be as soon as this fall. And I am already contracted to Lûn."

"I would not ask you to break *that* contract," Ilanz said, with a little emphasis on that. "What's pushing them to do it now?"

"My spies in Valdaire, and my ears among the troops, say you are too popular… You've taken in fugitives from both cities, have you not? And you have prospered; population's grown. They expected you to fail."

"And do they know about this?" Ilanz pointed to his better eye.

"Yes. They think the lion is toothless as well as blind. They fear both your success and the chaos that may follow when you fall."

Ilanz held himself stiffly, unmoving, hands spread on the map. "And your counsel is that Aesil and I should leave quickly, before the trap is weighted? For I see no safety in surrender." He'd always known this day, this fate, might come, but he kept staring at the map he could not see, for the escape that did not exist.

"There is none, Ilanz: as you said, they want you dead and your city razed. You can escape as a single man or with a small band—"

"Ah, old friend, *you* will understand what I say now. I have a contract." Halveric said nothing; Ilanz went on. "A contract with the people of Margay, the people who were here, being abused by Vonja. A promise to protect them to the end of my life. I will not leave. Aesil will go—"

"No!" Her young voice, full of passion.

Ilanz had expected that. "Squire and captain of mine— daughter I never had—you *must* go. What use to anyone if you die in this? Some of my men will go with you; you can start a company with a few. I did. Get to Valdaire; work with Lord Halveric. You still have that crystal, do you not?"

"Yes, but—"

"Aesil, you are a M'dierra, not a Balentos. Dragonkin. You have a heritage of honor. I never did, nor your father—"

"He's a witward—"

Ilanz made a rude gesture. "*Witwards.* Stay away from them, Aesil. Your father is not a bad man, but like me, he came from— Never mind what. Be my heir."

He heard the weakness in his own voice. Aesil would hear it; it would tempt her to stay for his sake. She must not.

He went on. "Remember what you told me about being taken to Horngard as a small child? The dreams you had for days afterward?"

"Yes, but—"

"Don't *die* for me, Aesil," Ilanz said. "*Live* for me. Live out my legacy. Shine golden as the sun."

"What kind of niece leaves her uncle to be hacked up by thieves?"

"A niece who knows she can protect his legacy, his soldiers still able and willing to fight—not here, not now, but later. You would have inherited my company at my death. Inherit it now, and make it glorious."

"Andressat will take you in," Halveric said again. "What use for you to stay here alone to die?"

"A contract." Ilanz smiled again. "I will try to make my death serve them."

Halveric nodded. "I could wish you were not as good a man as you are; I will miss you. You taught me more about honor than I knew back then. I will go ahead to Cilwan, tell the Count what's afoot, then tell Andressat your heir will come." He looked at Aesil; she nodded.

"If the trap is not yet weighted, there might be a way to save more—" Aesil's voice held no emotion.

Ilanz smiled to himself. She had that ability, thank the gods, to set emotion aside and think clearly. Ilanz had seen it before, one of the rarest and most important talents for a commander.

"Any evacuation will draw attention," Halveric warned. "You're in sight of the Guild League road: they will have spies."

"Yes, my lord," Aesil said. "But that road—" She must be pointing out something other than the Guild League road. "*That* goes to Cortes Cilwan. If Andressat is our ally, didn't you say last year Cilwan was theirs?"

"Cilwan is Andressat's ally, yes. Related by marriage a generation or two back, and by a betrothal expected to lead to another marriage in a few years. Yes. And there is a way… not so much a road as a drover's route marked with waystones, south from Cilwan and then west to Andressat. And regular messengers between them." The Halveric captain looked at Aesil. "That's a good idea."

"Just a few at a time," Aesil said. "Families from here trade both north to Sorellin and Ambela, and south to Cortes Vonja, then west to Valdaire."

"Yes," Ilanz said, his expression shifting. He had, with the shock of Halveric's news, forgotten Margay's best cash crop. "All those dyers and weavers up there—Sorellin's pride, their fine woolens. Excellent. But it takes our people right into the danger. They'll be arrested—"

"Not this time of year. We'd be sending fleeces in both directions in the next ten days anyway; our people are shearing now. Sorellin won't suspect. Add in Cilwan, because we do have a lot of fleeces held back. And they don't have to stay long. Visit any family members, do a little trading, just as usual, and on the way back, they're coming from Sorellin, not from here; they can pass by, head for Cortes Cilwan without suspicion."

"You have another problem, though," Halveric said. "Spies."

"As you said, watching the road—"

"That too, but more important, spies here, in the town. My squire found one when I sent him to that good bakery on your square. With spies as with rats——if you see one, you've got more. If you had no internal spies and your people had any discipline, such a plan might work."

He paused.

"My people have more discipline than most civilians," Ilanz said. "Not as good as my troops."

"That might be enough, without the *embedded* spies," Halveric said. "For this to work, you'll have to be able to find them, deal with them in the next day or so. Already, some of them will know I've been here."

"Yes. Aesil, that's first, before we let anyone know of the other plan."

"Then—if I understand what Aesil was thinking," Halveric said, "very small groups of civilians, each with a soldier or two, taking fleeces to market, could likely pass as normal seasonal movement. Both civilians and soldiers could trickle away on pretense of making another trip. You've a small population—what is it, about a thousand? You might even get most out. It'll be harder as the population drops to hide the loss. As for soldiers, as we all know, they cannot walk a road together any distance without falling into step, marching along. They'll be watching for that."

"Lord Halveric, you are right," Aesil said. "We must start now, tonight, to locate the spies. And with much careful thought." Ilanz could hear the change in her voice. "Where is that spy you found, Lord Halveric?"

"Downstairs, being interviewed by one of your uncle's captains."

"Good. He must not leave this house alive." She turned to Ilanz. "My lord, with your permission, I will carry your word to your captain."

Ilanz reached for her hand; she gave it. "No longer a mere captain. You have been the light of my aging, Aesil, before this. Now you have had a good idea I should have seen for myself. We will spend this night planning, you and me and Aliam, and *you* will decide things. It is in my heart that you *will* find a way to save most. They do not have all their forces in place yet. We have a chance."

"Yes, Commander. I'll see to this first." Aesil hurried down the stairs.

"Will she kill him?" Aliam asked.

"Yes, or order it. Quickly as she can, as we discussed."

He knew Aliam would try again to get him to leave. It was not an argument he'd wanted to repeat while Aesil was in the room. "I *can't* go, Aliam. You will understand. I had a contract with my people. From the start. This is not their fault. I'm staying. Even if most of them leave; I know there are men of mine who will stay even if I go. *I* stay."

"To die."

"To die, yes. As all do. In the place I wanted to die; you should look at it that way. I will die thinking, even if I cannot say, like your Falk, *I kept my oath.*"

"A close-run thing it will be, if you can accomplish it, Ilanz."

"Worth it," Ilanz said. He felt a surge of energy. "And there's a cellarful of most excellent drink, for those who want it."

"I count you as a true friend," Aliam said. "And all your advice has been good for me. I—"

"You saved Aesil from that jail. You saved both our companies, at our first encounter here." He switched topics, hoping to divert Aliam from another attempt. "How is your redheaded former squire? Did you send him to Falk's Hall, as you said you would?"

"Yes."

"In confidence, at this our last meeting, knowing I will not reveal anything you say… who do *you* think he might be?"

Aliam's voice lowered. "I thought perhaps he might be our prince, child of our former king and his elven wife. He was lost, his mother killed, as they traveled, his body never found. By looks, as he grew, he could be. By intelligence, skills… but elves have seen him at my steading—they come every winter for a visit— and said nothing to me. Surely, *they* would know. He himself has shown no sign that he remembers anything useful before waking in captivity. So, when he wins his ruby, I will send him out of Lyonya, make sure he doesn't go to court, where his resemblance to our young queen would be too obvious and likely cause a stir. I'll continue to do what I can for him without betraying her; she should make a good queen as her lineage is not in question. His, if the elves never proclaim it, will always be clouded."

"You saved his life, and with your patronage, you will ensure him a career. You are a fine man, Aliam."

Halveric snorted. "I am a mercenary. Fine men live in fine houses and wear fine clothes."

Ilanz laughed. "We will not speak more of that. I hear her coming back."

"Commander," she said as she came into the room. "May I report?"

"Go ahead. Aliam won't mind."

"He owed money to a merchant in Vonja; he went there to pay it off and was threatened that his son would be attacked if he didn't spy for them. I told him we'd take care of his family." Aesil took Ilanz's hand. "I sat with him, said I'd tell his wife. He was brave at the end."

"Good," Ilanz said. "There's one more thing. When you have your company, whenever that is, I want you and Aliam to carry forth the pact he and I talked of—to recruit other companies to a pact of honor, to treat one another's troops well, no matter what employers say. Maybe a formal registered Guild but at least a private pact. Promise me."

"Yes," Aesil said. "I promise."

"I witness," Aliam said. "I have spoken to Count Vladi; we have an agreement between us. With Aesil, that will give us three, and if Kieri comes back, as I expect, after he's got his ruby—"

Ilanz held up his hand. Blind as he was, he knew every scent of night air: it was time for Aliam to leave, to get away safely. "Aesil, go down, tell one of the house guards to open a gate quietly." She moved away and down the stairs.

"It's time, sir." Aliam's captain said, turning away from the window. "Stars dimming."

Ilanz felt Aliam's warmth near him, then Aliam's hand clasping his. He rose, and they hugged hard, pounding each other's back for a moment. Ilanz spoke first, as the elder.

"Old friend. Dear friend. Go now, and the gods give you joy, long life, and many children."

"I have many children already; Ilanz,. It's why I have to come down here to fight for a living." Aliam's voice was firm. "Fare well, Ilanz, as long as you can, and gods give you an easy death and a banquet in the stars."

They hugged one last time, and Aliam left the room. Ilanz felt tears on his own cheeks and swiped at them. He sat back down, listening. Boots on the stairs, on the floor below and other voices, then silence. Aesil came back after a time, as the light grew to a grey blur in the window.

"They're gone," she said. "I need to talk to the captains."

"Do that," he said. "And if the kitchen's ready, I'd like sib and morning bread. In the garden." He picked up his stick and moved slowly to the stairs. She needed to do this herself; he knew she'd killed the spy herself, though she hadn't said so.

Aesil M'dierra summoned Ilanz's oldest captains, three of the five, to her uncle's office. When they arrived, dawn's light colored the world outside as if freshly painted. Ilanz was not there.

"How is he today?" asked Fortnis, seniormost. "His eye?"

"Captain, he will tell you when he comes. What I tell you

now, he has instructed me to say. Commander Halveric brought dire news. Margay will be attacked with overwhelming force, likely before Midwinter. Sorellin and Vonja have made common cause." Clear morning light made it easy to see every shade of expression on their faces. All looked as usual.

"How did Halveric know this?" Fortnis asked.

"Rumors in Valdaire and on the road to Lûn. But here is what else I know. A spy was found in town here. We now know he was working for Vonja, having been threatened with harm to his family. He is dead; he will tell no more tales. But there's always more than one. Have any of you noticed anyone behaving strangely?"

And there. The flicker of eyelid, the sideways shift of the eye beneath it she'd been waiting for. Rordanil, junior of the three senior captains, whose father, she recalled suddenly, was a witward of Pliuni, like hers.

"Rordanil," she said, "how long have you been with the Count?" She felt the other two captains come alert, though neither of them moved.

"Fourteen years."

"And before that?"

"Four, in Pliuni's City Guard."

"Your father's a witward, the Count told me; so is my father. They probably know each other."

Another flicker of eyelid. "He is; I know he knows Witward Balentos. They're in different fincana."

Aesil pulled the crystal dragon on its chain out of her shirt. "You know what this is?"

Sudden sweat glistened on his face, obvious in the merciless sunlight coming level through the window.

"Yes." She pulled the chain over her head. "Here—have you

ever held one? Harmless to truth-tellers…"

"It's not fair!" His voice was a tone higher. "You're just a girl; you'll get us all killed. The Count put family over the welfare of the Company. It should've been Fortnis or me."

She heard a sound from Fortnis; a glance silenced him, but she met both captains' eyes briefly. "You think envy's an excuse for betrayal?"

"It's not an excuse, not envy. It's the truth. *You* can't command a company. We have to look out for ourselves." He glanced at the others, clearly hoping for agreement, and met stony faces.

"Betrayal is betrayal," Aesil put the chain back over her head and dropped the amulet into her shirt.

"You *can't* kill me," he said, stepping back, hand reaching for his sword hilt. Fortnis and Murandan grabbed his arms and looked at Aesil.

"What's your will, Commander?"

"Bind him, take him to the cellar, put a watch on him. I'll tell the Count; he may want to speak to him."

In the garden, Ilanz felt his way to the bench under the north wall, where some roses still bloomed, their scent heavy on that sunny day. He drank the sib a servant brought and ate one of the sweet breakfast rolls from the basket the cook had sent. His mind still churned, but he also felt lighter. The load was being lifted, the darkness lightened, the way ahead clearer every handspan of day. He heard Aesil coming down the steps and raised a hand to her.

"Which was it?"

"Rordanil."

"Ah. I'm not surprised. What have you done with him?"

"Cellar, with Fortnis and Murandan."

"Did he say why?"

"It wasn't fair, you setting me over the captains; he respected you until I came. You placed family over the welfare of the Company. The Company should have gone to Fortnis as the senior."

"Rorda always was a whiner and conniver. If I hadn't gone blind, I'd have gotten rid of him years ago."

"Yes. His father knows mine, did you know? Another witward."

"I knew, yes," Ilanz hadn't thought of that connection for years. "I knew him from Pliuni. We weren't friends as boys, but his family did a business with mine. You know how it is. One of my visits home, we had a bowl together at Mika's on the Square, and he said he was unhappy in Pliuni's Guard troop. Asked about hiring in Valdaire. I'd just lost a good captain to swamp fever down south of Andressat." He sighed. "I hired him. Long before your time, Aesil. Vladi was still attached to Horngard then, I think. That was before Sofi Ganarrion came South. Vladi wore a kilt, if you can believe it."

She couldn't. Nor did she care what someone had worn thirty, forty years before. "About Rorda—"

He grimaced. "Yes, of course. Will you let me talk to him? I have some connections that might get him to tell us something useful."

"Of course."

"I'll go in now. Shouldn't take long. I can find my way to the kitchen from here. Go down and have Fortnis meet me there; I don't trust myself on cellar stairs."

"Do you want your sword? Or would you like mine?"

"No need." Ilanz's smile did not reach his eyes. "Has the first party left with fleeces yet?"

"I'll find out," Aesil said.

"Remind them to mention that if Sorellin doesn't want all our fleeces, we'll be taking them to Pler Vonja and even Vonja. And make sure any household goods in their wagons are well hidden."

Rordanil refused to divulge anything more; the execution was swift.

Fortnis and Murandan fetched the other captains. Ilanz interviewed them, with Rorda's body forming a clear and present warning.

All passed as true, with Jeris, the youngest, mentioning a visitor from Pler Vonja who had been found in the fleece cellar and escorted away, and the boys who'd led him down there. "He bribed them with coin. Copper only. The boys are just eight and ten. They didn't see anything wrong with answering a merchant's questions and bragged to him about all the fleeces we'd already sheared. Their father's one of our wool dealers. Bardon."

"Travels to Sorellin?"

"Yes, my lord."

"I'll want to speak to him. A ten-year-old should know not to take strangers into the cellars; if his father's not taught him merchant caution—"

"Yes, my lord, I'll fetch him in."

It was the wool dealer's wife, whose three sisters in Sorellin had sent her gifts from there—ostensibly from her uncle—for years, sent notes thanking her for helping the family anticipate how many fleeces they would have. She'd told the boys to take her uncle's employee to look at the fleeces.

Ilanz's stomach griped. Kill a woman, a mother? Her husband, distraught, begged mercy for her. "She meant no harm. And what harm could come just from knowing how many fleeces?"

Fortnis stirred.

Ilanz shook his head. "A great deal of harm could. I trust that you meant no harm and she meant no harm, but I have many others to protect. I cannot let you stay."

"We can go to Sorellin—"

"No. You will leave today; I will lend you two men to help you pack and hitch your team. You will go to Valdaire—you go every other year—"

"But not now. We go in spring—"

"You will leave *today* for Valdaire, with an escort to be sure you have no trouble on the road. You will say you are looking for a new market for our fleeces; you're unsatisfied with what Vonja and Sorellin pay. You will not stop overnight in Vonja territory, and when you stop in Foss Council towns, you will not let your wife or sons talk to anyone there. Say it's a Guild matter. I also require you to visit my banker in Valdaire on an errand; it will be a sealed packet given to you on arrival in Valdaire."

"But—but our house, our things—"

Ilanz managed not to sigh aloud. Civilians were so slow to catch on. "Bardon, you have only this choice. Either you go today, with your family, to Valdaire, with what fits in your trade wagon, or I must kill your family to save others. I can promise if you choose death, it will be quick and as easy as possible. But the wise choice is exile. Never return."

Within two turns of the glass, Bardon and family were packed and on the road, escorted by two of Ilanz's soldiers, in uniform. His wife had quit protesting after she was brought to Ilanz's house to see Rordanil's body.

"They're my sisters," was all she'd said, almost a whisper, her face white as salt. "Just family. Please don't hurt them. I didn't know."

149

"I won't, as long as you stay in Valdaire or south of there and don't talk about Margay business." Ilanz turned to Bardon. "You have your funds?" The man nodded.

Five more spies broke and ran for it over the next two days, all caught and executed quietly.

After the "last rabbits" were taken, Ilanz and Aesil talked to the Company and the Margay town council, explaining the evacuation measures. Ilanz then talked to his Company and the town leaders. After the initial shock of being told there were no alternatives, evacuation began promptly. Six families who had already loaded their wagons with fleeces went first, four to Sorellin and two to Pler Vonja, their wagons festooned with bunches of fall flowers. By then, word had come from Cilwan that both soldiers and civilians could be welcomed there. The first trade wagons to Cilwan carried the former Company's rolls, and the Margay records as well most of Ilanz's remaining gold, to open an account in Margay.

Day by day, the numbers of civilians and troops within Margay dropped, slowly but steadily. The more adventurous chose to go back and forth between Sorellin, Ambela, Pler Vonja, and Vonja several times, carrying fleeces one way and money the other. Money deposited with the local bank every time they came through, when they would overnight in their own home and take a few more things out of it on the next trip. Everyone whose final destination was Cilwan took their money in coins. When the last wagon went to Cilwan, it would clear out the local bank and banker.

Ilanz convinced Aesil to leave early, to be a liaison in Cilwan. He suggested where to go after Cilwan and Andressat, how to approach Valdaire later with a full company in existence. He signed an introduction and gave her the codes she would need to access his funds there.

The less adventurous made but one trip, to more destinations or waypoints: Cortes Cilwan, Lûn, Andressat, Foss Council cities, even Valdaire. The only ones who stayed in any of the three "enemy" cities had relatives who were citizens of long standing.

As houses emptied, the remainder spread into them, lighting fires every day so the amount of smoke above the town would look normal. Every day and night, guards marched along the walls, and every day, a guard troop left the gates to walk the inner bounds, as usual.

So, by the time ten hands of days had passed, Margay's civilian population was no more than thirty, and the real number of troops was about the same. It was harder to furnish the daily guard troop for the walls, for walking the bounds, even with the soldierly of the civilians helping. But they had the satisfaction of knowing they'd sneaked out almost the entire population and most of what the invaders would consider plunder.

Those still in the city did not intend to leave. The blind, like Ilanz, the very old, the lame, those who simply dreaded leaving a familiar place for uncertainty. And Ilanz's oldest soldiers would not leave their commander behind, helpless.

"If we could just destroy the buildings in one night, and leave them nothing—" one old man said.

"Too much work. We built it too well."

"We'll have a feast," Ilanz said. "Plenty of food left: cook for a hundred, sixty of us can finish that."

"How many days?"

That discussion lasted only two days. Ilanz had sent Fortnis up the highest tower, the roof of his house, every night, without a light, to look for clues to the enemy's movement. The second night of the discussion, Fortnis came down and reported seeing campfires closer in than the camps Halveric had found. "And I heard dogs barking at the outlying farms. Gods grant our farmers weren't all killed."

"They're near enough the outbound markers they'll just take the land from them," Ilanz said. "I hope. Go tell our cooks to get the ovens going; tomorrow we feast. Tomorrow night—"

"We die," said Balanis, another blind man. "We do have plenty of wine, right? And something to put in it?"

"Both," Ilanz said. "And frustrate them all to hellpits." He had thought to talk to Fortnis first and privately, but all sixty-three were there, waiting for his word. "We're cut off now," he said "It's only a matter of a day or two. I have one last trick to play."

He took a small leather pouch out of his pocket and shook the contents into his hand by feel. He heard some indrawn breaths, silence from the others, as they saw what lay in his hand. A small crystal dragon on a thin gold chain. "I'm not *true* dragonkin—this was not given to me by one of Dragon's priests. I stole it off a dead man decades ago because I knew what it was. But I also learned the Curse of Camwyn's Claw. And there are dragonkin in my family background. Maybe Dragon will be merciful and honor the curse."

"It kills—" Murandan started.

"The one who calls that curse down, yes. But it usually destroys the target, if Dragon agrees. I have held it and prayed to Dragon every night since Halveric left. I will cast that curse tonight, after our feast, and *I* will certainly die—but if it works, those of you who want to live may be able to escape. You know Aesil will accept you, and she will need your experience. And you will know if it works; you can tell her."

"How will we know?" Jeris asked.

"Fire in the sky," Murandan said. "Maybe even see Dragon. I heard both. My lord—"

"My mind is set," Ilanz said. "Better Dragon kill me than a Vonjan. Only choice left. One last chance to honor my oath to my people."

Cooks laid the feast out on tables from various houses the next morning: hams, beef roasts, loaves baked that very day, some still warm from the oven, fancy rolls filled with chopped nuts in honey and spices, redroots and spiced grain, bowls of butter, custards using the last of the eggs and cream and flavored with spices and chopped apples. Enough for twice the number still in the city. Up from the cellars the strongest had wrestled barrels of beer and wine, so the feasting began before noon and carried on all the afternoon, until all were full and more than full. The stone bottles of poison Ilanz had promised sat on a separate table to one side, but only a few poured some in their cup with sweetened wine and went off to a house to die before the others. Most waited for dark.

When it was full dark and growing late, and and talking and singing had replaced eating and drinking, Ilanz and his senior captains went up the stairs in his house, all the way to the narrow passage to its roof. They brought along a hurdle; Ilanz nodded when they told him. "Yes, it will be awkward getting my body down. Or you could just throw it into the garden from up here, you know."

"We will not," Fortnis said. He sounded shocked. "We honor you, Commander."

Ilanz took the pouch out again, shook out the crystal dragon figure. "I need your help to aim the curse," he said. "I cannot see where those camps are, or the watchfires. I will hold this in my hand, aiming at them, and you must turn me so I have pointed at all of them while speaking. Squeeze my arm if you need me to talk slower."

He felt two of them taking his arms, steadying him and he lifted his arm with the crystal in his hand and began with a prayer. "Lord Dragon, though I am not rightfully dragonkin and stole this amulet, I beg you to help my people by enacting this curse on our enemies. Camwyn Dragonfriend, I call on you." And then he began the curse itself. To his astonishment, his vision cleared, both eyes seeing the glow of fires in the distance, and as his men turned him, and continued, the sky overhead lit with a burst of fire and then streaks of it racing across the sky: one, two, three, four, five, six such streaks, breaking into lesser streaks, and as he finished, and drew another breath… a blow like an axe to his chest, a moment's pain, and he fell.

Fortnis saw the streaks of fire, and above them the figure of a dragon glowing golden. Where the streaks came to the ground, fire rose to meet them, and a short time later, the sounds of explosions, screams, from all the places they'd seen watchfires or knew there were underground camps. The explosions finally ceased, night grew quiet again, but the distant flames did not go out.

"Well," he said. "We'd better get our Commander down to his garden and decently buried."

"In the dark?" Murandan said. "Can't we wait until morning?"

"I have a feeling," Fortnis said. "And an idea he would have liked. We'll take lanterns."

After the burial where Ilanz had wanted, the group dispersed, some to take poison with sweet wine, some to sit with their friends until dawn, some to sleep, as Ilanz had suggested. In the morning—a quiet, foggy autumn morning—those who had chosen death had died, and those who chose life poured all the remaining oil and wine over the corpses and the town, in every house, on every stick of wooden furniture, and set it all alight.

Then Fortnis led them out, their packs stuffed with food and anything else they wanted. They came through the town gates a last time and walked on, leaving the gates wide open.

A chill wind blew on them from the north, and within the first half-day of walking, winter's first snow fell, one flake after another, and then a flurry.

Far away, seated at the Andressat table one evening, Aesil M'dierra felt the sudden heat of her crystal dragon against her skin; her hand rose to it even as the Count of Andressat stopped in mid-word. "You, too?"

"Yes, Sir Count," she said. "But I don't know—"

"Someone has invoked the Curse of Camwyn's Claw," he said. "Did your uncle—was he dragonkin?"

"Not that I know," Aesil said. "He never said anything to me."

"It is like him, nonetheless," the count said. "A man of honor, though neither wise nor of noble blood."

AUTHOR'S NOTE ON "DESTINY"

Also in *Deeds of Youth*: the story "Consequences" introduced Kieri Phelan again as a young mercenary captain with his first independent command, military advisor to the Crown Prince of Tsaia, marching toward the Pargunese invasion force. Now, four hands of days later, than the end of "Consequences," Tsaian nobility demand a Tsaian tradition: a banquet before battle. The outcome will determine Kieri's entire future… and Kirgan Marrakai's as well.

Aliam Halveric sponsored Kieri to Falk's Hall for knights' training, so by the time he earned his ruby—but did not take it at first—Kieri was twenty-two winters old. He was the top knight-candidate in his class, his success assumed to result from the training Aliam had given him in Aarenis. Kieri then went to Aarenis to start his own mercenary company, and over the next four years as a subcontractor had gathered a full cohort of his own, met the Crown Prince, and impressed him as competent beyond his years. The Girdish nobles of Tsaia, however, saw a young man without known family—no breeding—and Falkian rather than Girdish. Foreign-born, foreign-trained. Some of them had doubts until his true identity was revealed decades later.

Publication history: "Destiny" is new, written exclusively for *Deeds of Wisdom*.

DESTINY

Kieri Phelan, Fox Company captain and putative military advisor to the Tsaian army expedition, finished his inspection of his single cohort. As always, they stood ready for his command, should the enemy attack.

He wished he could say as much for the whole Tsaian army.

Siger, his sergeant, said it for him. "*We're* ready. The rest of 'em are ready for a banquet, not a battle. Are these fools trying to get killed?"

"Not 'these fools,'" Kieri said. "Our employers." No sarcasm; he had raged internally earlier in the day. Now he thought only of what he could do, would do, in the trouble he knew was coming. "They lack experience of war," he said; Siger knew that, but Kieri wanted his own calm to seep into Siger and his soldiers. His troop's discipline, their ability to resist the panic and excitement of the locals, was crucial. "We have a few allies—"

"Lads," Siger said. "Too young—"

"Kirgan Mahieran is a knight—"

"Underage, though."

"True, but I have hopes of Selis Marrakai. And his friend, the Serrostin boy, will follow his lead. And several Marshals and their granges."

"Trained for a war five hundred years past."

"Disciplined, though."

Siger sighed. "I hope so, sir. I agree the Marrakai lad's changed for the better, and his father's grateful, so I really hope he remembers what we—"

"So do I," Kieri said. "I think he will, and he's influenced his friends to wear basic armor. We won't break; we can hold and attract other units of Tsaians to join us. We do have the numbers to drive them back."

"If you're in command," Siger said. "If it's one of these nobles?"

Kieri tipped his hand back and forth. "Crown Prince, Duke Mahieran, Duke Marrakai, yes. Others—I'll be there. Should work. Three tendays ago, maybe not. But now, the enemy's shed several parties taking loot back to Pargun. If they attack tonight, I'll wager it's in hope of scaring us back, to give them an easy escape."

Siger nodded and turned away.

Kieri looked after him, thinking of the arguments he'd lost in the past two days. His plan would have kept them safe, but some of the nobles had convinced the prince he was too cautious as well as too young. So, no triple line of defense, no picket line covering flanks and rear of their camp. He had argued against the planned banquet, the concentration of important personnel in one place. Tradition demanded it, the Crown Prince had said.

And if the enemy did attack and did kill the commanders, what was he expected to do? Command the army, win the battle, drive the Pargunese back over the border, and then take the blame for their losses when they returned to court. He'd faced that possibility squarely.

* * *

160

Selis, Kirgan Marrakai checked his appearance in the mirror again, tightened his sword belt, and smoothed the fall of his short green cape with red braid around the margin. He ignored the sound of a gong in the distance.

"Selis!" His father the Duke's voice broke into his worry that something—a hanging thread, a tiny spot—marred his appearance. "It's time."

A final glance at the mirror, a final pass of the comb through his hair. "Coming, Father." He left his small chamber in the tent and found his father just hanging his own sword, wider and longer than Selis's, on his belt.

His father wore breast and back with the Marrakai crest emblazoned on the front, a longer cloak, and carried his helmet under his arm, its red feather trailing up over his shoulder.

His father's usual hard gaze softened into a smile.

"You look very well, Selis," his father said. "Quite soldierly, I may say. You've grown up a lot on this trip; I'm proud of you." He cleared his throat. "Tomorrow—"

Tomorrow, when the armies fought, when his father would command Marrakai troops on the field.

"You'll be safe enough," his father went on. "You'll all have horses; if there's a problem, just head for home." He nodded shortly. "I know you'd rather be with me, but you'd need knight's training for that. What you've learned from your mercenary captain is not enough, though it's done you good."

Selis did not argue, as he once would have.

Outside, his father waved to Duke Mahieran, the King's brother, just emerging from his tent across the way.

The two dukes fell into step, heading for the command tent; their kirgans followed.

"Selis." Sonder, Kirgan Mahieran, greeted him. As a royal,

Sonder had been admitted to the Bells early and wore the spurs and insignia even though he was only a year older than Selis. "And there's Erdo," he said, indicating Duke Verrakai's kirgan up ahead. "They're splitting us tonight, you know," he said. "Even though we'll be watching the battle with you youngers tomorrow, as your protection, tonight we'll be on the sword side of the table. Finally."

Selis struggled with his temper. *"Don't go looking for insults and quarrels,"* Phelan had told him. *"Anger is a good weapon but a bad master."* He and his father caught up with Duke Serrostin and his kirgan Tollyan. Tolly and Selis, best friends, grinned at each other. Selic let his irritation with Sonder's tone go. It didn't matter, really, what Sonder said. Sonder would be on the other side of the tent, across the big tables, unable to nudge him if he and Tolly said something.

Erdo stood beside his father, Duke Verrakai. Duke Elloran and his kirgan Rodanif stood a little apart. Dani, youngest of the kirgans present, only twelve, looked anxious. He had no close friends among the older kirgans, and hadn't trained with them. The Elloran domain was far to the south, backed up to the mountains that cut off the Eight Kingdoms from Aarenis, and even Duke Elloran came to Valdaire only for official duties. When the Crown Prince came down the lane between tents, the crowd gave way. He wore armor like the other men, mirror-bright, the Tsaian rose on his breastplate, helmet under his arm.

He nodded to the dukes and their kirgans. "Well on time, gentlemen," he said, as if he had not doubted they would be. "Let's go in. An early meal, early to bed, and early rising to battle and victory."

"To victory," they all answered. The Prince led the way into the tent. A long table stretched to hold the dukes, the younger prince and his personal guard, select invited counts, while lesser lords—barons, counts, and kirgans—stood either side. Tonight, a steward indicated the younger kirgans should turn heart-hand around the table, and the elder, the newly knighted turned sword-hand, where they could put men's swords in racks set up in rows between the table and the tent wall to the north, and retrieve them later.

The younger ducal kirgans, Selis, Tolly Serrostin, and Dani Elloran, moved toward the foot of the table, followed by lower-ranking kirgans, and stepped back until the tent wall was at their backs. The space between them and the table filled with counts and barons; Selis caught a glimpse of the younger prince standing behind the center seat of that short end between two of the Royal Guard on his sword-hand and Captain Phelan and one of his mercenaries on his heart-hand.

Phelan's gaze crossed Selis's and paused, then he nodded at Tolly Serrostin next to him and frowned slightly at Dani Elloran. Selis looked at Elloran again. Now he noticed the younger kirgan's breast-and-back fit loosely, and his sword had a decorative loop around the hilt and through a ring on the scabbard, like a child's sword. Had his father not trusted Dani to leave his sword sheathed? Finally, all the adults had found their places and waited for the Crown Prince. He sat down at the end, Verrakai on one side of him, Mahieran on the other, Serrostin and Marrakai on the corners. The rest took their seats.

Phelan's warning came back to Selis, along with instructions. *Breathe. Listen. Draw only on my order. Parry first.* Selis donned his helmet as Phelan had recommended. To his surprise, so did the other kirgans, even Elorran. He felt his sword hilt, twitched it. Yes, loose enough. Tolly glanced at him. "Just checking," he said.

The Prince signaled, and servants brought in platters of

food; rich scents of roast boar and beef, great dishes of redroots, steamed grains in gravy, stewed spiced fruit filled the tent. Servers brought in more, and more, and the men were talking now, mostly about what they wanted.

"Does he think something's going to happen?" Tolly asked, learning close. "Your Captain Phelan?"

Selis shrugged as if they discussed nothing of importance. "He said be alert, that's all. Be sure my sword was easy to draw but not to draw without orders," repeating what he'd told Tolly the day before.

"Anything else?"

"Listen. For anything unusual. An attack makes noise."

"And does the little commander have other orders for us?" That was Count Konhalt's kirgan, on Selis's other side. Flaris, that was his name.

"No," Selis said, ignoring the tone of contempt. "Just do what's necessary. If he signals, I'll say draw sword."

Flaris Konhalt's expression shifted to surprise.

What had he expected Selis to say? Selis tried to think what Phelan might tell them to do if something happened.

Protect the royals?

The Crown Prince was too far away; the younger prince already had protection. Try to hold back the Pargunese? With a single line of Barons and kirgans?

Try to get to his father?

If only there'd been Phelan's soldiers just outside as they'd been other nights. But not this night.

Servers came by with trays of finger foods for those standing. Selis, mindful of what he'd been told and the uneasy feeling in his midsection, took only a few bites of pastry-wrapped meats and sipped water from the goblet offered. The men ate quickly, and servants began clearing the table.

Men talked louder.

Barons stepped closer to the table, leaving their sons near the tent wall. The light, Selis realized, had dimmed a little; it wasn't dark, but sun no longer poured down on the tent. When the table was clear, six men brought out the battlefield model and laid it on the bare table.

Servants went around the tent, lighting lamps hanging over the table. Selis couldn't see the model through the adult backs, but he'd seen it before. Outside the tent, the camp had quieted but for the sound of servants carrying away the dinner service.

Listen, he reminded himself. Someone stumbled; dishes scraped on a tray and clattered to the ground; some broke. One servant cursed another for clumsiness.

Normal sounds.

The Prince was talking, pointing down the table. Far off, a fox barked. Then a horse neighed in the horse lines. And another.

The horses had been fed. They should be eating, not neighing. Selis looked toward Phelan, who met his gaze. Then he heard running, many feet on the ground, and someone yelled "Fire! Get water!" Others called out, questions, orders, some words he didn't know.

Phelan nodded, a sharp jerk of his head, and spoke loudly. "Distraction! Swords!" Phelan stood up, sword in hand, and met Selis's eyes. "Draw swords!" Others froze where they were, staring at him. A few pushed back, stood.

The signal. Draw. Selis felt cold suddenly; his stomach clenched. The noise outside grew, more shouts of fire, calls for water.

"Draw sword," Selis said to Tolly and Flaris Konhalt, even though they must have heard. He pulled his sword up three fingers, four... "Tell Dani—"

Suddenly, even-louder noise from outside. Whistles screeched, animal sounds—howls, roaring, words shouted in a language he did not know.

Selis yanked his sword free, but before he could pivot, he heard canvas ripping and felt a hard blow on his back plate. Selis whirled with it, as he'd practiced with Phelan's sergeant, parrying the blade aimed at him, steadying Konhalt with his other arm as Konhalt got his sword free barely in time to parry.

More Pargunese pushed through the slashed tent, forcing Selis back, into the men behind him.

Now more noise and chaos as Tsaians yelled orders, cursed, bumped into each other and the line of kirgans as they tried to get to the sword racks beyond the table. Selis felt battered by the noise, confused by the mass of men in front of him, all armed, all the sharp points and edges coming at him. He parried frantically, already out of breath, backing until the table rim struck him behind. He could feel the rings of his mail shirt through his clothes.

He and Tolly fought stroke and stroke with the men that faced them.

The enemy's broad red faces and yellow beards could have been Girdish peasants. Their black shirts and helms weren't. His helmet cut off his side vision; he heard Konhalt on his heart side, grunting with every stroke.

Tolly's sword on his other side danced almost in time with his own. Behind him, from the end of the table, he heard Phelan signal his troops, three piercing notes sharp as a blade, and an answering roar from up the lane between the tents. Then more attackers shredded the curtains at the servants' entrance and rushed in toward the low end of the table—and the younger prince.

"SELIS! SHIFT SWORD-SIDE!." Phelan's voice, now from overhead.

Phelan was up on the table? Why? Had the Crown Prince called him?

He glanced up automatically and missed his parry. From overhead a sword slashed down, caught his enemy in the face; the man stumbled back, quickly replaced by another.

Selis parried the new attacker's blade, caught his own rhythm again. Then he bumped Tolly with his hip; they both pushed sideways, shoving, bracing against the table, fighting their way to the corner.

He caught a glimpse of the Royal Guardsman at the corner falling. Only the Royal Guard captain remained on this side of the young prince, and his dagger arm was bloody to the shoulder, his hand empty, dripping.

Tolly parried a sword aimed at the captain; Selis forced his way around the corner, parrying with sword and dagger.

Beyond the young prince, a Fox Company soldier held a shield over the prince's torso, and parried with his own sword. A baron had come around the far corner to help. But where were Phelan's troops? All Selis could see were the Pargunese massed between him and the servants' entry and the side wall where he'd been.

His shoulders ached, his fingers cramped on the hilts of sword and dagger.

Finally, Selis heard Siger, Phelan's sergeant, calling cadence to the Fox Company unit just outside the shredded canvas of the servants' entrance, and the response Selis had heard all summer, loud and firm. *HO—HUH! HO—HUH!* They pushed through, a solid block of shields and swords. The Pargunese in the rear ranks turned, not fast enough; their rear rank fell and the second rear staggered back into those still facing the table. Selis had no time to be amazed; he fought harder, parrying blow after blow from multiple swords. Tolly lunged forward, but a Pargunese in front of him slipped his parry and one swipe severed Tolly's sword hand. Selis drove his own blade home in the man's neck.

A wedge of Fox Company soldiers broke through to the table end. One grabbed Tolly's wrist, shouted, "DOWN," and Tolly fell where he stood.

Another pushed Selis toward the young prince. "Get him under the table."

Selis grabbed the prince and swung him down and around, startling them both.

"Safer under, my lord," he said to the prince, leaning down with him. Around and behind them, the clash of swords and the noise went on. Stray blows thudded into the table end. He heard someone walking on the table, the thump of boots landing where he'd been standing.

"I've got them," the Fox soldier said from underneath, and, "Prince, squeeze here, hard."

Selis eased back and stood up again.

He felt shaky; he wanted to stay under the table himself. Siger was looking at him; Selis stood, breathing hard. *Alive*, he thought. *I'm alive.* He looked around. Already the Pargunese had been driven halfway out of the tent, and the fight was moving toward the ripped entrance near the head of the table.

Siger tilted his head toward the other end of the table, gestured.

"Kirgan Marrakai, you're needed. Up on the table; go to the front. Captain wants you."

Before he could protest, two Fox soldiers grabbed his arms, lifted, helped him up onto the table. From that height he could see the wreck of the battlefield model, smears of blood, fresh gashes in the wood.

The baron he'd been fighting beside waved to catch his attention. "Kirgan Marrakai!" Selis waved back, then pointed to the far end. Bodies on the trodden grass below, some moving feebly. He fixed his gaze on the upper end. The Crown Prince had his head down on the table; surely, he wasn't sleeping? Beside him, Duke Mahieran leaned sideways and blood glistened on his surcoat, redder than the embroidered roses. Then was the Prince—? As he neared the end of the table, he saw the Prince was dead, his head cleaved, and so was Mahieran. Verrakai? He could not see Duke Verrakai—or his father. He took another step, to the table's end, looked down.

His father lay below. Two men in Marrakai livery looked up and quickly covered his father's wounds with a cloth that turned red at once. His father had worn only the short upper breastplate of a mounted fighter and not the taisse like Selis.

Selis shuddered. He had seen slaughtered cattle.

He felt himself sagging, falling, could not stand... One of the men stood abruptly, grabbed him, and swung him over and down, holding him up facing away from his father. "There now. You're bleeding too, young lord. Breathe."

He breathed. It was harder, much harder, but the air came in, and after a few moments, he shook his head. "I—I won't fall."

"Right. Jarin, stay with the Duke. I'll get the young lord to the captain. Breathe, young lord. Deeper, if you can. You've fought well, I can see. Air's fresher out here. Is the—is the young prince still—"

"Alive," Selis said. "Tolly and I—then Tolly was hit. They're under the table, I think." Suddenly, that seemed funny, and his next breath came out in a great "HAW!" Phelan, just outside the tent opening, turned to look at him.

"Marrakai! I need you."

No time to laugh or cry, no time for anything but to walk, at first unsteadily with the familiar livery beside him, and then steadily, ten steps, twelve. Outside, the sky was still bright, though no direct sunlight but one narrow beam, glinting on the helms and armor of a struggling mass, Royal Guard and Pargunese, and a mass in Marrakai uniforms milling uselessly, clearly uncertain what to do.

"Captain," Selis said, past the lump in his throat, the need to spew.

"Marrakai," Captain Phelan's voice was loud enough to reach him but calm. "Your troop needs you. I know you can lead them. They know you. That man on this side is your father's—now *your*—senior sergeant. Go say, 'Sergeant, I am taking command.' Tell him to support the Royal Guard's flank."

Selis wasn't sure the man would obey; he hadn't even started in the Bells yet. But something in Phelan's steady gaze, those clear grey eyes, settled his gorge, let him take another longer breath.

Phelan was sure... he could do it; Selis walked toward that sergeant.

Took a deeper breath and with it remembered the man's name as well as the Old Language command words his father had taught him.

"GRASTI VAKONY! Sergeant Vakony! FORM UP— DAAKINZO! Follow me!"

Vakony turned, stared. "Young lord! Yes, my lord! DAAK- INZO!" The milling mass settled, turned toward him. "DRESTAT!" Selis raised his sword, realizing for the first time just how much blood was on it, seeing blood streaks wet on his arm. He looked at the other. On both arms. His dagger was red from tip to pommel. The Marrakai hurried into ranks. He walked past them, calling "VROST! VROST!", directly toward the rose and white formation of the Royal Guard, his sword held high. And they followed.

He felt the surge of confidence Phelan said came with command. These *are* my men. *My* people. Doubt of his ability left him as he heard them close behind.

He let out a yell of exultation and rage, and his men roared behind him.

Sonder Mahieran, his royal colors splattered with blood, grinned at him as the Marrakai troop closed on the Royal Guard flank. "Marrakai! *Now* we can move." Selis nodded but stayed focused on the enemy. He felt no fear, no excitement now but grim determination.

More quickly than Selis had expected, the Pargunese lines softened.

A distance opened between their lines and the Tsaians.

Kieri Phelan watched carefully as the Pargunese attack weakened, then retreated slowly down a shallow slope, harder and harder to see in the gathering darkness. The Marrakai boy's courage had made the crucial difference. Too bad his father wouldn't live to know it.

His own cohort protected the Marrakai flank; to his own right was a Girdish group. Beyond Mahieran, the colors of Konhalt and Serrostin, then more blue.

Now a little distance, widening, separated the two forces. Then from the Pargunese, someone yelled a phrase that sounded like Pargunese Kieri had heard during a riot near the docks of an Immerhoft port: *End fight!*

He yelled, "Halt! All halt!"

The noise diminished slowly as others echoed that command. Kieri waved a torchbearer nearer.

A single man, barely visible in the dimness, stepped forward, holding his sword up vertically, point down. He stopped, lowered the sword to the ground, and pushed the tip in until it would stand on its own. He let go and stepped back, then spoke.

"Talk is?" the man said, in barely intelligible Common.

"What's what?" Mahieran asked.

"He wants to parley," Kieri said. "I have a little Pargunese."

"You talk, we listen," Kieri said in Pargunese, quickly translating for Mahieran.

The man answered in Pargunese, simply. "We go away. We take hurt men. We take dead men. Ask for mercy."

Mahieran cocked his head at Kieri, who answered. "They will go away; we can insist on all the way to Pargun. Should be close now. They want to take their wounded and their dead. That means having them around another day, but I say we should agree."

"They attacked us. They invaded us, burned farms—"

"I know. But they're beaten now, and their leader is dead. Depending on who it was…"

"That man is king?" the Pargunese asked.

"No," Kieri said, with the head-jerk the Pargunese used. "Not king. King's brother-son. You killed our king's oldest son."

"You kill our king's brother, the Sagon."

"Two princes dead," Kieri said, to be sure.

"Yes." The man bowed stiffly but low. "Is no war-tribute rank on each side equal."

"I will ask. King's brother also died."

"Two princes your side, one our side. We owe—"

"I will ask."

Kieri explained it to Mahieran. *Duke* Mahieran now; did the young man realize that yet?

"Two kings' brothers, one king's son," Mahieran said. "A sad day for both sides. Two dukes, four counts who never reached their swords, three barons. If only those"—he nodded at the Pargunese—"had stayed home. Why did they invade, can you find out?"

Kieri asked that question. The man shook his head, said something complicated Kieri couldn't follow, though he caught the words *god* and *no food make hungry* and *new king*. Then the man asked, "How do you speak Seafolk?"

"I fought in Aarenis," Kieri said. "I met Pargunese in Valdaire and Immerdzan. I speak it badly." He thought about mentioning his own brief childhood experience with Seafolk but decided it had no relevance there.

"Not so bad. We look for hurt men now?"

Kieri looked again at Mahieran, who sighed and said, "This is beyond me. I have a father and cousin to mourn, and the... the rest. Just make sure we aren't attacked again."

"I believe this man is honest," Kieri said. "I would allow them two small groups, under our guard, to search, and assign sentries and watchfires..."

"Yes. You know what to do. I am suddenly out of... everything."

No wonder, Kieri thought, and bowed. Mahieran turned to the Royal Guard ranking officer. "Do what Captain Phelan advises."

"Yes, my lord Duke."

As Kieri had expected, Duke Marrakai did not regain consciousness before he died, though he lived another two days. He paid his respects; the boy was tight-lipped and merely nodded when Kieri visited, then muttered, "Thanks," before turning to the next visitor. Kieri also expected the summons from the King for all commanders to come directly to the palace while the army was still several days' march away. Riding through the night, no one chatted; Kieri himself felt a bleak certainty that the King would either kill him or send him empty-handed back to Aarenis.

They were all led upstairs to a room Kieri had never seen before, where a man in royal livery told them what to do. Then he summoned Kieri. "The King will see you first," he said. "Come with me."

Kieri followed as the others straggled toward chairs and a table set to one side. Finally, he was ushered into an obvious office, with a desk on a dais. The King, seated behind it, nodded at the other man, who left, closing the door. One chair stood on the lower floor across the desk from the King, with a small table near it, with a pitcher of water and a fancy-looking glass. Everything in the room looked expensive, from the frieze of tiles with a hunting scene that ran around the ceiling, to the thick deep rose carpet edged with paler rose-pink flowers. Kieri bent the knee and bowed. The king's face might have been carved in stone, he thought, a stern, unyielding countenance.

With reason, he thought. Hired as the military advisor, he had cost this king a son, a brother, and three dukes in total. Of the ducal kirgans, one was dead and another missing his sword hand. More noble youths lost among the counts and barons, because he had not convinced the Crown Prince of the need for more caution.

He was not like to have the chance to make that mistake again.

Of course, he would not receive the grant the prince had promised and cleared with the king. He would go back to Aarenis with the remnant of his hundred men, disappointing Aliam, and try to claw his way through the ranks of more experienced mercenaries until, perhaps, he gathered a cohort or two more and made enough to support them. Resigned to failure, he stood easily under the King's regard, past fear or resentment or anything but quiet respect.

"Captain Phelan, pour yourself some water, then come and sit down. I have many questions for you. I imagine you have anticipated many of them."

Kieri sat where he was bid. "Now," the King said, "your letter to me was remarkably detailed about the sequence of events, very clear, but your explication of motives and tone was far less so. I take it as understood that the attack on our force was sudden and effective, but so was the response, and the Pargunese had not numbers enough to defeat. They depended entirely on surprise. Had you anticipated such a plan?"

"Not exactly when it came, sir king. But yes, I anticipated a surprise attack. Other evidence had convinced me that their numbers were less than ours."

"How did you come to that conclusion?"

Kieri explained what his scouts had reported and what clues indicated the size. "This doesn't determine the actual strength of each force; that depends on their fighting qualities. How well trained, how fit, how recent their prior fighting experience." He paused, the King's gesture asked more. "A small, well-trained, fit force can give up size to a larger force that's unfit, less well trained, and either lacking recent-enough experience or exhausted by too-recent combat. The Pargunese miscalculated and let too much of their force go home early."

"Did you find our army unfit, untrained?"

"Some units, yes. Ideally, troops train year around. Not all the noble lords, nor even all Marshals, require the same amount of training. They have other priorities, other things that must be done for their own welfare and that of the realm."

"I see," the king said. He continued to ask intelligent questions about the army, which Kieri answered. He asked why the Pargunese attacked in the first place.

"If I understood the man, they had two bad harvests and were short of food. Their new king, quite young, was told by one of their gods they could move west and take the land so people would not go hungry. Their own land, they say, is not as good for farming. They thought you would accept the god's word and cede them the land."

"Arrogant," the king said, confidently, as if arrogance were entirely a foreign vice.

Kieri held his peace and hoped his feeling that Tsaians were as arrogant as their enemies did not show. He liked them, the ones he'd met—well, most of them—but despite the Company of Gird's emphasis on equality and simplicity, this very chamber displayed signs of pride and wealth, from that frieze of southern tiles fired with gold in the glaze to the carpet spread on the dais beneath the throne and the gold leaf worked into the intricately carved arms and back of the king's chair.

The king went on to lead him through the sequence of events again, this time asking which decisions were his, who and when others had opposed them, and insight into their motives. And then how Kieri knew what he related of these things.

"Among so many, in any company, there are those who take pleasure in sharing what others do not want shared," Kieri said. "Of course, it is just what I understood of what they said. I don't know them well enough to know if they understood the other persons, or if they were being accurate."

The king actually laughed, short and quietly. "Captain, I can well believe you were trained by Lyonyans. I suppose it's living among elves so much."

"Possibly," Kieri said. "They do speak precisely when they speak. At least in our languages."

The king shook his head and went on to ask about the late Crown Prince and the younger one.

"The Crown Prince and Duke Mahieran were killed instantly when the Pargunese forced the entrance at the head of the table, axe blows to the head, as they were not wearing helms. I ran up the table after giving the alarm but was too late to save them."

"You were at the foot of the table with Haris?"

"Yes, sir king. With one of my men; the Royal Guard captain and a guardsman were on his other side. When I went up on the table, seeing what had happened, Count Lorton came around the corner to help my soldier protect Haris."

"Go on."

"Prince Haris fought bravely. Kirgan Marrakai and Kirgan Serrostin came to his aid just as the Royal Guard commander, already wounded, was killed. My troop broke through the Pargunese cordon outside and into the tent shortly before Kirgan Serrostin lost his hand, and got both the kirgan and the prince into cover, where Haris and one of my men stanched Kirgan Serrostin's bleeding stump while the rest of my troop cleared the tent. Young Marrakai, despite seeing his father near death at his feet, and his own wounds from earlier, came with me and rallied the Marrakai cohort; he and Mahieran commanded the nucleus of the victory."

"And your troop did nothing? Be not too humble, Captain Phelan."

"They were magnificent, sir king, but they had the advantage

177

of long training. My sergeant, Siger, had five campaign seasons with Halveric Company before he came to me, and four since. He had the men in the right place at the right time, and when I called, they answered. That is the professional advantage, the years and the hours of preparation. It taught me; it saved the day there, I will say that proudly."

"Good for you." The King nodded. "Now here's my command. You will return to the army to collect your men, and go directly north to busy yourself with your new possession. I want you out of the way—so far my nobles cannot cause you trouble—while I grill them and we all mourn what was lost and celebrate as we can what was saved. You may have two nights here—in the city, not the palace—to gather what you need and go. You had a fee promised; I will send a draught to the bank at the corner of Market and Palace. You will need tools, I suspect, and rations and such. Get them fast, and get out before the rest of the army arrives, which I'm told will take another three or four days. You will have orders to show the Royal Guard commander, but do not stop to chat; is that clear?"

Clear as a pond horses had romped in, Kieri thought. The king wanted him gone, but he was still getting the grant? And the money?

"Thank you, sir king," he said, out of his confusion.

"The snows will be too deep for you to come back for Midwinter Court," the king said. "So, your investiture as Count Phelan will take place at the Spring Evener. I will send more details by courier before the weather's too bad. You will need to come down by half-spring to arrange for your investiture robes."

He had not imagined needing court regalia. He had thought—the Crown Prince had said—he would hold as a baron first, possibly even baron-elect for a couple of years. Count?

"Or have one of the listed tailors take your measurements now. It will not hurt your reputation if their apprentices leak to someone that your robes are already being made. In fact, I recommend Fingan, by appointment to the Crown, two blocks down Market. He knows all the details. Maroon and white and— you want that fox head for your emblem?"

Kieri couldn't think for a moment. That fox head one of his men had sketched, become the heraldry of a Tsaian lord? A—a COUNT? He blinked against the sting of tears. "Sir king—"

"And you'll pledge fealty. Again at the ceremony, of course, but I must have your pledge now as well. Come up here. Kneel and give me your hands."

Kieri knelt, mind still whirling.

A man with no family. Someone's bastard, undoubtedly. On his knees in front of a king, his hands clasped in the king's, pledging fealty, as a lord to his higher lord, about to have a tailor embroider his emblem on some kind of ceremonial regalia? And— He repeated the words the king had said, realized the king had already drawn his own sword and felt its weight laid on one shoulder and then the other.

"And get yourself a horse. A good one" was the last thing the king said before "Dismissed, my lord Captain Count-to-be." He had a mischievous look in his eye that Kieri had seen and liked in the Crown Prince's.

Kieri bowed again; the king rang a small bell. A man in uniform led Kieri out a complicated way into a hot afternoon, in the courtyard of the Royal Guard stables, where a double-gate opened into the street.

ABOUT THE AUTHOR

USMC veteran Elizabeth Moon is the author of many novels, including *Echoes of Betrayal, Kings of the North, Oath of Fealty,* the Deed of Paksenarrion trilogy, *Victory Conditions, Command Decisions, Engaging the Enemy, Marque and Reprisal, Trading in Danger,* the Nebula Award winner *The Speed of Dark,* and *Remnant Population,* a Hugo Award finalist. After earning a degree in history from Rice University, Moon went on to obtain a degree in biology from the University of Texas, at Austin. She lives in Florence, Texas.

THE

TENTH
ANNIVERSARY
EDITION

SPEED

ELIZABETH MOON
WITH A NEW INTRODUCTION BY THE AUTHOR

OF

DARK

A Novel

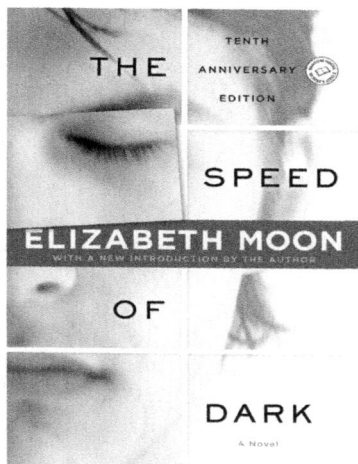

**Winner
2003 Nebula Award
for Best Novel**

**Finalist
Arthur C. Clarke Prize
for Best Novel**

Perfect for your next book club selection

In 2004, *The Speed of Dark* was selected for Kansas City's "United We Read" initiative. Since then, it has been used for campus reading events at Ohio State University, Clemson University, and Suny Oswego. It has also been a part of community events for library systems in Howard County, Massachusetts, and Georgetown, Texas.

This book is part of the Random House Reader's Circle collection and comes with a discussion guide that makes it the perfect choice for any reading group.

"Inevitably, *The Speed of Dark* has been compared to Daniel Keyes' classic and tragic Flowers for Algernon, in which a mentally disabled young man is medically enhanced to become a genius. *The Speed of Dark* may be an even greater book…; it is [a] subtle, eerily nuanced character portrait of a man who is both unforgettable and unlike anyone else in fiction … It is a measure of Elizabeth Moon's genius that she enables a reader to thoroughly experience the world through Lou's tangled but exhilarating neurology, and wonder what we "normal" people are missing when we don't acknowledge our connection to those who seem so different from us. A lot of novels promise to change the way a reader sees the world; *The Speed of Dark* actually does."

– Elizabeth Hand,
Washington Post Book World

"A touching account. Well-written, intelligent, quite moving. Moon places the reader inside the world of an autistic and unflinchingly conveys the authenticity of his situation."

– *Kirkus*, starred review

FOR NEWS ABOUT JABBERWOCKY BOOKS AND AUTHORS

Sign up for our newsletter*: http://eepurl.com/b84tDz
visit our website: awfulagent.com/ebooks
or follow us on twitter: @awfulagent

THANKS FOR READING!

*We will never sell or give away your email address, nor use it for nefarious purposes.

Printed in Dunstable, United Kingdom